"A remarkable story."

"An enchanting, imaginative account."

—*Spirituality & Health* magazine

"Malinalli is a prism through which we can also glimpse what it is about Laura Esquivel's sensibility that has made her a bestselling novelist."

—*Hispanic Magazine*

MALINCHE

Laura Esquivel

Translated by
Ernesto Mestre-Reed

Illustrations by
Jordi Castells

WASHINGTON SQUARE PRESS

New York   London   Toronto   Sydney

Washington Square Press
1230 Avenue of the Americas
New York, NY 10020

The Library of Congress has cataloged the Atria hardcover edition as follows:
Esquivel, Laura, date.
    Malinche: a novel / Laura Esquivel; translated by Ernesto Mestre-Reed; illustrated by Jordi Castells.
        p. cm.
    Includes bibliographical references.
        1. Marina, ca. 1505–ca. 1530—Fiction.   2. Cortés, Hernán, 1484–1547—Fiction.   3. Mexico—History—Conquest, 1519–1540—Fiction.   I. Title.

    PQ7298.15.S638M35 2006
    863'.64—dc22
                                                            2005057124

ISBN-13: 978-0-7432-9033-3
ISBN-10:   0-7432-9033-X
ISBN-13: 978-0-7432-9035-7 (Pbk)
ISBN-10:   0-7432-9035-6 (Pbk)

First Washington Square Press trade paperback edition April 2007

10   9   8   7   6   5   4   3   2   1

Manufactured in the United States of America

For information about special discount for bulk purchases, please contact Simon and Schuster Special Sales at 1-800-456-6798 or business@simonandschuster.com.

To the Wind

MALINCHE'S CODEX

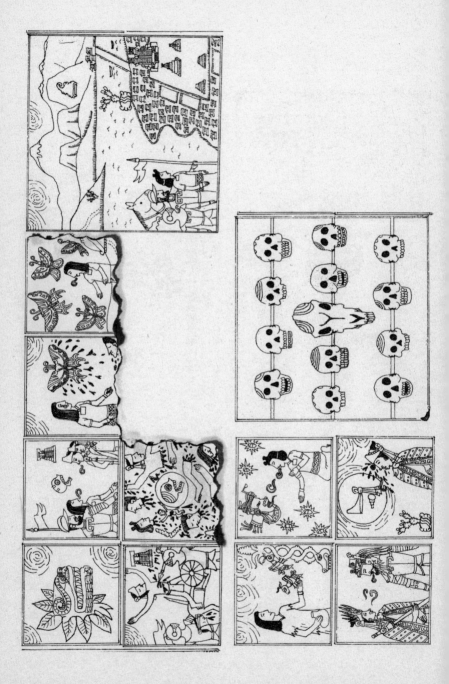

AUTHOR'S NOTE

To enter what was—or what may have been—the world of Malinche, proved to be a fascinating experience: to imagine the stars she gazed at, what her favorite flowers were, what food she liked best, what it meant in her daily life to light a fire, what gods she turned to in times of anguish. And I soon realized that the image she probably had in her mind of any god, would have come from a codex or a sculpture.

The history of the civilizations that inhabited the American continent before the arrival of the Europeans, the memory of the tribe, was preserved either by oral tradition or through images, not through written language. The ancient Mexicas told the epic poems of their people through images. All their experiences were recorded on pieces of paper that represented a way of existing in time. Those documents were called codices and their creation was so important, as much in the artistic conception of them as in the material realization, that the "writers" of codices were considered superior beings and their activities sacred. In fact, they were exempted from paying taxes to the state, so fundamental was their work considered in the culture of pre-Hispanic America.

The codices preserved all the knowledge of the pre-

Columbian civilizations. From those that were spared destruction, we can come to know the images of the gods or the history of the emperors, their forms of tribute and of healing, all the way up to the most heartrending chronicles dealing with the arrival of the Spaniards, with the falls of empires and the process of conquest. The codex was a sacred mode with which to tell stories, profane and holy stories. And so the codex symbolizes a process of mediation, it unifies the mental effort to explain events rationally with the artistic and religious experience of expressing the world emotionally and spiritually through concrete images full of color and whimsical shapes.

Some historians have asserted that the most important image for cultural reconciliation of the Spanish conquest of American lands is that of the Virgin of Guadalupe. She has been conceived and imagined as one of the most sophisticated forms of the codex. In each of the brushstrokes of "The Dark Lady of Tepeyac" there exist coded languages that were understandable only to the Mexica people, though in no way could you ignore the interpretations that were addressed to the Spaniards, the criollos, and the race of mestizos that we now justly call Mexicans.

For these reasons, I thought it essential that this novel be accompanied by a codex, the codex that Malinche might have painted. The codex would represent what the words narrate in another fashion. In this manner I try to conciliate two visions, two ways of storytelling—the written and the symbolic—two breaths, two yearnings, two times, two hearts, in one.

MALINCHE

ONE

First came the wind. Later, like a flash of lightning, like a silver tongue in the heavens over the Valley of Anáhuac, a storm appeared that would wash the blood from the stones. After the sacrifice, the city darkened and thunderous eruptions were heard. Then, a silver serpent appeared in the sky, seen distinctly from many different places. And it began to rain in such a way as had been rarely seen. All afternoon and evening it rained and through the following day as well. For three days the rains would not cease. It rained so hard that the priests and wise men of Anáhuac became alarmed. They were accustomed to listening to and interpreting the voice of the water, but on this occasion they insisted that not only was Tláloc, God of Rain, trying to tell them something but that by means of the water he had allowed a new light to fall over them, a new vision that would bring a different meaning to their lives, and although they did not yet clearly know what it was, they could feel it in their hearts. Before their minds could correctly interpret the depth of this message that the waters revealed as they fell, the rains stopped and a radiant sun was reflected in myriad places among the small lakes and rivers and canals that had been left brimming with water.

That day, far from the Valley of Anáhuac, in the region of Painala, a woman struggled to give birth to her first child. The sound of the rain drowned out her groans. Her mother-in-law, who was acting as midwife, did not know whether to pay more attention to her daughter-in-law about to give birth or to the message of the god Tláloc.

It didn't take long for her to decide in favor of her son's wife. It was a difficult delivery. In spite of her long experience, she had never been present at such a birth. While washing the mother-to-be in the bathhouse just prior to the delivery, she had failed to notice that the fetus was in the wrong position. Everything had seemed to be in order, yet the anticipated birth was taking longer than usual. Her daughter-in-law had been naked and squatting for quite a long while and still couldn't deliver. The mother-in-law, realizing that the unborn was unable to pass through the pelvic channel, began to prepare the obsidian knife with which she cut into pieces the fetuses that could not be birthed. She would do this inside the wombs of the mothers, so that they could easily expel them, thus sparing at least their own lives. But suddenly, the future grandmother, kneeling in front of her daughter-in-law, saw the head of the fetus poke out of the vagina and then shrink back a moment later, which probably meant that the umbilical cord was wrapped around its neck. Then, just as suddenly, a small head poked out from between its mother's legs with the umbilical cord caught in its mouth, as if a snake was gagging the infant. The grandmother took the sight as a message from the god Quetzalcóatl, who in the form of a serpent was coiled around the neck and mouth of her future grandchild. The grandmother quickly took the opportunity to disentangle the cord with her finger. For a few moments, which seemed like an eternity, nothing happened. The hard rain was the only sound that accompanied the moans of the young mother.

After the waters had spoken, a great silence took root and was broken only by the cries of a young baby girl whom they named Malinalli, since she was born under the third sign of the sixth house. The grandmother shouted like a warrior to let everyone know that her daughter-in-law, a great fighter, had come out victorious in the battle between life and death. She pressed the granddaughter to her bosom and kissed her again and again.

Thus the newborn, daughter of the Tlatoani of Painala, was welcomed into her paternal grandmother's arms. The grandmother sensed that the girl was destined to lose everything so that she might gain everything. Because only those who empty themselves can be filled anew. In emptiness is the light of understanding, and the body of that child was like a beautiful vessel that could be filled to overflowing with the most precious jewels—the flower and song of her ancestors—but not so that they would remain there forever, but rather so that they could be remade, transformed and emptied anew.

What the grandmother could not yet understand was that the first loss the girl would experience in her life was far too soon at hand and, much less, that she herself would be strongly affected by it. Just as the Earth had first dreamed about the flowers, the trees, the lakes and rivers on its surface, so had the grandmother dreamed about the girl. The last thing she would have thought at that moment was that she could lose her. Witnessing the miracle of life was powerful enough to prevent her from dwelling on death in any of its manifestations: abandonment, loss, disappearance. No, the only thing her body and mind wanted to celebrate was life. So the grandmother, who had so actively participated in the birth, looked on joyful and spellbound at how Malinalli opened her eyes and shook her arms vigorously. After kissing her on the brow, she placed her in the arms of her father, the Lord of Painala, and proceeded to carry out the first ritual after a birth, the cutting of the umbilical cord. She did it with an obsidian blade that she had prepared just for the occasion. The blade had been polished with such care that it seemed more like a resplendent black mirror than a knife. At the moment of cutting, the piece of obsidian captured the rays of the sun filtered through the thatched roof and their intense reflection was focused on the grandmother's face. The magnificent rays of the solar star knifed into the grandmother's pupils with such force that they irremediably damaged her sight. At that moment she thought that maybe this was the meaning of the reflections, a coming nearer to the light. She also understood that in helping her daughter-in-law give birth she had become a link in the feminine chain created by countless generations of women who assisted each other in childbirth.

The grandmother then carefully placed the child at her mother's breast so that she could be welcomed into this world. On hearing her mother's heartbeat, the girl knew she was in the right place and stopped crying. The grandmother took the placenta outside to bury it by a tree in the courtyard of the house. The ground was so heavy with the rains that the burial was made half in earth, half in water. The other half of Malinalli's umbilical cord was drowned in the earth. With it, life was sown anew, returning to the earth of its origin. The cord that binds the earth with the heavens ceded nourishment to nourishment.

A few days later, the grandmother herself baptized the girl, for tradition stated that the midwife who had brought the child into the world would have that honor. The ceremony took place at sunrise. The girl wore a *huipil*, a traditional sleeveless dress, and tiny jewelry that the grandmother and mother had personally made for her. They placed a small clay washbowl in the middle of the patio and next to it arranged a small trunk, a spindle, and a weaving shuttle.

In beautifully decorated ceramic stoves they burned copal. The grandmother carried a censer, and directing it toward the spot where the sun was beginning to rise, she spoke to the wind:

"God of the Gusts, stir my fan, raise me to you, lend me your strength, lord."

In response, a light breeze grazed her face and she knew that it was the right moment to make her greeting to the four winds. She turned slowly toward each of the four cardinal points as she said her prayers. Then she swung the censer under her granddaughter, who was being held high in the air by her parents, as they offered her to the wind. The small figure, silhouetted against the blue sky, was soon blanketed with copal smoke, a sign that her purification had begun.

The grandmother put the censer back in its place and, taking the child into her arms, raised her again to the heavens. She then dipped her fingers in water and let the girl taste it.

"This is the mother and father of us all," she said. "She is called Chalchiuhtlicue, Goddess of Water. Take her, let your mouth receive her, for you will need her in order to live on this earth."

Then, dipping her fingers in the water again, she touched the child's breast.

"See here, for she is the one who will enable you to grow and revive, the one who will purify you and will make your heart and your insides thrive."

Finally, using a calabash, she poured water over the girl's head.

"Feel the freshness and greenness of Chalchiuhtlicue," she said, "who is always alive and awake, who never sleeps or dozes, may she be with you and embrace you and keep you in her arms so that you will be awake and resolute on this earth."

Immediately afterward, she washed the child's hands so that she wouldn't be a thief and her feet and her groin so that she wouldn't be lustful. Finally she asked Chalchiuhtlicue, Goddess of Water, to cast out all evil from the body of the child, to set it aside and take it with her. Then she concluded by saying:

"From this day forward you shall be called Malinalli, a name that will be yours alone, the one that by birth belongs to you."

To end the ceremony, Malinalli's father took her in his arms and said the customary words of greeting, in which he chanted the prayer of welcome given to newborns.

"Here you are, my awaited daughter, whom I dreamed about, my necklace of fine jewels, my quetzal plumage, my human creation, engendered by me. You are my blood, my color, in you is my image. My little girl, look on peacefully. Here is your mother, your lady, from her belly, from her womb, you were engendered, you sprouted. As if you were a leaf of grass, you sprouted. As if you had been asleep and awoke. Now you live, you have been born. Our Lord, the keeper of all things, the maker of people, the inventor of man, has sent you forth unto the earth."

At that moment, Malinalli's father felt an inspiration within him from somewhere quite different and instead of continuing with the traditional words of welcome, he mouthed a different chant.

"My daughter, you come from the water, and the water speaks. You come from time and will live in time and your word will live in the wind and be planted in the earth. Your word will be the fire that transforms all things. Your word will live in the water and be a mirror to the tongue. Your word will have eyes and will see, will have ears and will hear, will have the tact to lie with the truth and to tell truths that will seem like lies. And with your word you will be able to return to the stillness, to the beginning where nothing is, where all of creation returns to silence, but your word will awaken it and you will name the gods and give voice to the trees and you will give nature a tongue to speak for you of the invisible that will again be visible through your word. And your tongue will be the word of light, a paintbrush of flowers, the word of colors that your voice will use to paint new codices."

In the year 1504, when a young Hernán Cortés first set foot on the island of Hispaniola (nowadays comprising the Dominican Republic and Haiti) and realized that he had entered a world that was not his own, his imagination became filled with desires. Like a typical only child, he was used to having anything that he longed for. When he was growing up, he never had to share his toys with anyone and as a result was a capricious child who as soon as he wanted something would take it without hesitation. With such traits, it is not surprising that on discovering new lands his mind was overcome with ambition. He had arrived in

Hispaniola on his own, not owing allegiance to any army or religious order. What he brought with him, aside from delusions of grandeur and a yearning to see the world, was a desire for liberty. The persistent pampering of his mother had suffocated him and made him into a weak and sickly child. His adventurous spirit was a prisoner within the parental walls. Moreover, his parents' enormous expectations were an onus, a weighty burden that tormented him. He also felt that his parents, though they never told him outright, were disappointed with his short stature. He was not tall enough to join a cavalry or an army. So he was left with three options: to become a page in the king's court, to become a priest, or to train for a suitable profession. His father was never able to get Hernán accepted as a page, so that option was discarded. They found a place for him as an altar boy at the church, but he never made it past that position, perhaps because his character was not suited to serving God in such fashion. Ultimately, Cortés attended the University of Salamanca, where he learned Latin and studied law for a short period. On the lookout for fresh opportunities, however, he soon decided to lift anchor and set sail for the New World. He wanted to prove to his mother that he wasn't as small as she thought he was, and that he didn't need so much schooling to obtain money and power. He wanted to be rich, just like the nobles, who could do whatever they wished.

There in Hispaniola, the path his life would take depended on himself and himself alone. Almost as soon as he arrived he introduced himself to the Spanish rulers of the island, foremost among them, Governor Nicolás de Ovando and several of his close associates. In conversing with them he learned of the way of life in this new world and what it had to offer them. He didn't hesitate to suggest solutions to problems of governing, designing projects and then persuading them that he was the one who could carry them out.

Soon enough he had gained the trust and regard of the rulers, for not only had he succeeded in battles against the natives and helped to quell rebellions, but he had also designed routes and roads to cover distances in less time and in a much more secure fashion, as a result of which he was awarded a royal land grant of considerable value in a region where they planted sugarcane. For Cortés, this was not enough. His ambitious spirit wasn't satisfied. He wanted gold. All the gold he could get his hands on. He wanted to dazzle the world.

One morning, shedding the fear of always having to appear perfect, he decided to take off his boots—which added a little height to his short stature—and unfasten and cast off his clothes, so that he could feel his body just as nature had made it. He needed to rest his cracked feet, which during his voyage from Spain had become infected with various fungi that were difficult to treat.

The joyous prospect of walking barefoot in the sand motivated his spirit. The peace he felt that morning was so vast that he thanked God for his life and for the chance to live in such a historic period. Approaching the sea, he allowed the water to wash his feet and he felt immediate relief knowing that the water would purify his wounds the same way it purified the clothes of sailors on the high seas. During long seafaring trips, the only way to wash clothes was to bind them tightly inside a net that was cast overboard as the ship sailed on; the sea penetrated the fibers of the cloth, washed off all impurities, and left them completely clean. He remained there on the shore a long while, letting the waves wash his wounds. Staring off toward the horizon, he recalled the long days of his voyage when, overwhelmed on the ship's deck, he observed the sky and the stars until his mind opened and he understood for the first time the roundness of the earth and the infinity of the cosmos.

Later, when he emerged from the sea, he lay down in the grass so that his feet would benefit from the purifying rays of the sun. With one arm he covered his eyes to protect them from the midday light and let his mind relax. The distant sound of the waves lulled him to sleep for a moment. And that one careless moment was all it took for a venomous scorpion to sting him and release all its poison into his body.

For three days, Cortés struggled between life and death. They were days of rain and prayers. A powerful storm lashed into the island and it rained ceaselessly. Cortés did not even notice the thunder, and the Spanish companions who had helped him, listened to him, frightened by the things he said in his delirium. He spoke in Latin and other strange tongues. He told them that there was an enormous sun that continued to grow and grow, a sun that would explode and spread bloodshed everywhere. He said that human beings would fly through the sky without needing to rest on the earth, that tears and the unbearable stench of death would conquer all of his body. He pronounced the names of Moorish kings, spoke of the historic defeats of Spain, mourned the Crucifixion, entrusted himself to the Virgin of Guadalupe, shouted out curses and stated that it had been a serpent, a great serpent that had bitten him, a serpent that lifted itself up in the air and flew in front of his eyes. On and on he raved until he fell completely asleep. Some had left him for dead, and he seemed so peaceful that they made plans to bury him the morning after, but when they arrived there to proceed with the holy burial they found that Cortés had opened his eyes and miraculously recovered. Observing a transformation in him, they realized that his face radiated a new strength, a new power. They all congratulated him and told him that he had been reborn.

TWO

Malinalli had risen earlier than usual. All night long she had not been able to sleep. She was afraid. In the coming days, for the third time in her life, she would experience a complete change. After sunrise, they were going to give her away once again. She couldn't imagine what was so wrong with her deep inside that they would treat her like such a burdensome object, for such was the ease with which they dispensed of her. She made an effort to do her best, not to cause any problems, to work hard; and yet for whatever strange reasons they would not allow her to take root anywhere. She ground corn almost in the dark, lit only by the reflection of the moon.

Since the day before, when the songs of the birds had migrated, her heart had begun to shrink. In complete silence she had watched as the birds in their flight took away with them through the air a part of the weather, of light, and of time. Her time. She would never again see the dusk from that place. Night was approaching, accompanied by uncertainty. What would her life be like under her new masters? What would become of her cornfield? Who would plant the corn anew and harvest it for her? Would the field die without her care?

A few tears escaped from her eyes. Suddenly she thought of Cihuacóatl, the snake woman, the goddess also known as Quilaztli, mother of the human race, who at nights wandered through the canals of the great Tenochtitlán weeping for her children. They said that those who heard her could not go back to sleep, so terrifying were her mournful, anxious wails for the future of her children. She shouted out all the dangers and devastations that lay in wait for them. Malinalli, like Cihuacóatl, wept at not being able to protect her harvest. For Malinalli, each ear of corn was a hymn to life, to fertility, to the gods. Without her care what would become of her cornfield? She wouldn't know. From this day forward, she would begin to journey through a path that she had traveled before: being separated from the earth she had grown attached to.

Once again she would arrive at a foreign place. Once again be the newcomer, an outsider, the one who did not belong. She knew from experience that she would quickly have to ingratiate herself with her new masters to avoid being rejected or, in more dire cases, punished. Then, there would be the phase when she would have to sharpen her senses in order to see and hear as acutely as possible so that she could assimilate quickly all the new customs and the words most frequently used by the group she was to become a part of—so that, finally, she would be judged on her own merits.

Whenever she tried to close her eyes and rest, a twinge in her stomach would prevent her from sleeping. With her eyes wide open, she remembered her grandmother and her thoughts were filled with dear and painful images at once. Her grandmother's death had set in motion her first change.

The warmest and most protective affection that Malinalli

had experienced in her infancy was from her grandmother, who for years had awaited her birth. It was said that many times she had been at the brink of death, but would always recover proclaiming that she could not go until she knew to whom she would bequeath her heart and her wisdom. Without her, Malinalli's childhood would have been devoid of any joy. Thanks to her grandmother, now she could count on being resourceful enough to deal with the dramatic changes that she was facing and yet . . . still she was afraid.

To keep fear at bay she looked up at the sky for the Morning Star, for her dear Quetzalcóatl, always present. Her great protector. From the first time they had given her away as a very young girl, Malinalli had learned to conquer the fear of the unknown by relying on the familiar, on the brilliant star that would appear at her window and that she would watch as it slowly danced from one side of the sky to the other, depending on the season. Sometimes it appeared above the tree in the courtyard. Sometimes she saw it shining above the mountains, sometimes beside them, but always flickering, joyous, alive. The star was the only thing that had never abandoned her. It had been present at her birth and she was sure it would be present at her death, there, from its spot in the firmament.

Malinalli associated the idea of eternity with the Morning Star. She had heard the grown-ups say that the spirit of human beings, of all living things and of the gods, lives forever, not dying, but changing form. This idea filled her with hope, for it meant that in the infinite cosmos that surrounded her, her father and grandmother were as present as any star, and that their return was possible. Just as it was for Lord Quetzalcóatl. The sole difference was that the return of her father and grandmother would benefit only her, while the return of Quetzalcóatl, on the other hand, would alter completely the course of all the cities that the Mexicas had conquered.

Malinalli was completely opposed to the way in which they governed, could not agree with a system that determined what a woman was worth, what the gods wanted, and the amount of blood that they demanded for their survival. She was convinced that a political, social, and spiritual change was urgently needed. She knew that the most glorious era of her ancestors had occurred during the time of Lord Quetzalcóatl, and because of this she longed for his return.

Countless times she had thought about how if Lord Quetzalcóatl had never left, her people would not have been left at the mercy of the Mexicas. Her father would not have died and she never would have been given away. Human sacrifices would not exist. The idea that human sacrifices were necessary seemed perverse, unjust, and useless. So much did Malinalli long for the return of Lord Quetzalcóatl—the greatest opponent of human sacrifices—that she was willing to believe that her tutelary god had chosen the bodies of the newly arrived men in her region to give shape to his spirit, to house himself within them. Malinalli was convinced that the bodies of men and women were vehicles for the gods. That was one of the great lessons her grandmother had transmitted to her as, through games, she taught her how to work with clay.

The first thing Malinalli learned how to make was a drinking vessel. She was only four years old, but with great wisdom she asked her grandmother, "Who thought of having jars for water?"

"Water herself thought it up."

"Why?"

"So that she could rest upon its surface and tell us about

the secrets of the universe. She communicates with us through each puddle, each lake, each river. She has many ways of dressing up and appearing before us, each time in a new fashion. The mercy of the god who resides in the water invented the vessels from which, as the water quenches our thirst, it speaks to us. All the vessels filled with water remind us that god is water and is eternal."

"Oh," the girl replied, surprised. "Then water is god?"

"Yes, and so is the fire and the wind and the earth. The earth is our mother, who feeds us, who reminds us where we came from whenever we rest upon her. In our dreams she tells us that our bodies are earth, that our eyes are earth, and that our thoughts will be earth in the wind."

"And what does the fire say?"

"Everything and nothing. Fire creates luminous thoughts when it allows for the heart and the mind to fuse into one. Fire transforms, purifies, and lights everything we think."

"What about the wind?"

"The wind is also eternal. It never ends. When the wind enters our bodies, we are born, and when it leaves us is when we die. So we must be friends with the wind."

"And, uh . . ."

"You don't even know what else to ask. Maybe you should be quiet and not waste your saliva. Saliva is sacred water created by the heart. It should not be spent on useless words because then you are wasting the water of the gods. And listen, I am going to tell you something that you should always remember. If words are not used to water the memory of others, so that thoughts of god might flower, then they are useless."

Malinalli smiled as she recalled her grandmother. Perhaps she too would agree with her that the strangers had come on behalf of the gods. It had to be so. The rumors spreading from houses, towns, and villages confirmed that those bearded white men had arrived pushed by the wind. Everyone knew that Lord Quetzalcóatl could only be seen when the wind blew. What greater sign could be wished for as proof that they had arrived on his behalf, other than that they came pushed by the wind? Not only that. Some of the bearded men were crowned with golden hair, like ears of corn. How many times during their own celebration ceremonies had they dyed their hair yellow to become a perfect likeness of corn? If the color of the strangers' hair resembled corn silk, it was because they symbolized corn itself, the gift that Quetzalcóatl had bestowed on mankind for sustenance. Thus the golden hair covering their heads could be interpreted as a very propitious sign.

Malinalli considered corn to be the embodiment of goodness. It was the purest food you could eat, the strength of the spirit. She thought that as long as men were friends of the corn, food would never be lacking on their tables, that as long as they recognized they were sons of the corn that the winds had transformed into flesh, they would be fully aware they were all essentially the same and nourished themselves in the same way. There could be no doubt that those strangers and they, the natives, were alike.

She did not want to give thought to any other possibility. If there was another explanation for the arrival of the men who crossed the sea, she did not want to know about it. Only if they had come to reestablish the age of glory of her ancestors would Malinalli be saved. If not, she would continue to be a simple slave at the whims of her lords and owners. The end of the horror must be near. She had to believe that.

To confirm her theory, she had gone to a *tlaciuhque*, a fortune-teller, who read grains of corn. The man scooped up some grains of corn with his right hand. Then, with his mouth half open, he blew on them from the back of his throat and quickly cast them on a mat. Observing at length the manner in which the grains had landed, he was able to answer the three questions that Malinalli had put to him. How long will I live? Will I one day be free? How many children will I have?

"Malinalli, the corn is telling you that your time will not be able to be measured, that you will not know its furthest reaches, that you will be ageless, for in each period that you live you will find new meaning and you will name it and this word will be the path to undo time. Your words will name the yet unseen and your tongue will turn silently to stone and from stone, to divinity. Soon now, you will have no home and you will no longer devote yourself to making cloth and food. You will have to walk and watch, and watching you will learn from every type of face, from all skin colors, all differences, all tongues, of the things that we are, how we will cease to be, and what we will become. This is the voice of the corn."

"Is that all? It doesn't say anything about my freedom?"

"I have told you what the corn has spoken. I don't see anything more."

That night, Malinalli could not sleep. She didn't know how to interpret the fortune-teller's words. It was almost dawn before she fell into a sleep in which she saw herself as a great lady, as a free and luminous woman who flew through the air supported by the wind. That joyous dream suddenly became a nightmare, when Malinalli saw how beside her the Moon was pierced with daggers of light that injured her and set her completely on fire. The Moon then ceased being the Moon and became a shower of tears that nourished the dry earth from which unknown flowers bloomed. Malinalli, to her astonishment, named them for the first time, but she completely forgot about them on awakening.

⋘❈❂❈⋙

Malinalli took out a coarse cotton sack that she had tied under her blanket skirt in which were held the grains of corn that had been used to read her fate. It was a living memory that she would always keep with her. She had threaded the grains together with a cotton string to secure her fate. Each morning she would finger them one by one as she prayed, and this day was no exception. With great zeal she asked her dear grandmother to protect her, to watch over her, but more than anything she asked her to rid her of fear, to let her see with new eyes what was to come. She shut her eyes and tightly squeezed on the grains of corn before continuing her task. Drops of sweat dripped from her face, partly from the labor of working the grinding stone, but also from the great humidity that was palpable even at this early hour. The humidity didn't bother her at all; on the contrary, it reminded her of the god of water who was ever present in the air. She liked to feel it, touch it, but on this morning the wet air bothered her. It seemed to be charged with an unbearable fear, a dread that hid under rocks, under clothes, underneath the skin.

It was a dread that emanated from Montezuma's palace, which loomed like a shadow from the Valley of Anáhuac to the place where she was. It was a liquid fear that penetrated the skin, the bones, the heart, a fear caused by several terrible omens that had come to pass one after the other, years before the Spaniards had reached these lands.

They all foretold the fall of the empire.

The first omen was a burning ear of corn that appeared one night and that seemed to drip fire onto the earth.

The second omen was the conflagration that destroyed

the temple of Huitzilopochtli, God of War, for which no cause was ever discovered, no one having started the fire, and which no one was able to extinguish.

The third omen was a deadly ray that struck a thatched roof of the Great Temple of Tenochtitlán—a solar strike that came from nowhere, for it had been drizzling.

The fourth omen was the appearance in the sky of a mantle of sparks that, three by three, created a giant tunic which traversed the sky with its long train, originating from the spot where the sun rises and heading toward where it falls. When the townspeople saw it they shrieked in horror.

The fifth omen was the boiling waters in one of the lakes near the Valley of Anáhuac. The waters rose and boiled with such fury that they demolished all the nearby houses.

The sixth omen was the appearance of Cihuacóatl, the goddess whose wails could be heard at night. "My children! Where shall I take you? We must flee far from here."

The seventh omen was the appearance of an unfamiliar bird that some fishermen found and took to Montezuma. It was an ash-colored bird, like the crane, that had a mirror in its head; looking through it you could see the heavens and the stars. When Montezuma looked for a second time into the mirror on the bird's head, he saw many men fighting among themselves, and interpreted this as a dreadful prophecy.

The eighth and final omen was the appearance of misshapen creatures who possessed two heads, or who were joined at the front or the back, and who would disappear as soon as Montezuma noticed them.

Shaken, Montezuma called forth his sages and soothsayers.

"I want you to tell me what is to come, be it sickness, plagues, hunger, locusts, earthquakes; be it rains or no rains. Tell me! I want to know whether wars will be raged on us or whether deaths may result from the apparitions of mirror-headed birds. Don't keep it from me. I also want to know if you have heard the renowned Cihuacóatl crying, for when anything is about to happen in this world, she knows about it first, long before it comes to pass."

In the silence of dawn, Malinalli could swear that she heard the lament, the weeping of Cihuacóatl, and she felt an urgent need to urinate. She stood from her work at the grinding stone and went out to the patio. She lifted her blanket skirt and *huipil*, squatted and strained, but the liquid refused to leave her body. Malinalli then realized that the sensation in her belly came from fear and not from a physiological need. She missed her grandmother more than ever and remembered the day that they had given her away for the first time.

She was only a child of five. The thought of abandoning all that she treasured terrified her. She trembled from head to toe when they told her that she could take only what was absolutely necessary. She didn't have to give it more than a moment's thought, and grabbed a burlap sack, filling it with what her grandmother had left her: a jade necklace and bracelet, a turquoise necklace, some *huipiles* that her grandmother had embroidered for her, ceramic figures that they had made together, and some grains of corn from the fields that they had both harvested. Her mother took her to the outskirts of town. Malinalli, with her things on her back, clung to her mother's hand as if she wanted to become one with it. As if she, a mere girl, were the very Quetzalcóatl, struggling to fuse himself with the sun to govern the world.

But she wasn't a goddess and her wish was in vain. Her mother let go of her tiny grasping fingers, gave her away to her new masters, and turned away. Malinalli, upon seeing her go, peed on herself and felt at the moment as if the gods were abandoning her, that they wouldn't be coming with her, that the liquid that ran down her legs was the sign that the god of the waters had forsaken her. She wept the entire way, spilling her tears over the trails she crossed as if she were marking the path by which, years later, she would return, then in the company of Cortés.

The sorrow of that fateful day was greatly diminished when the following dawn, tired of weeping, she looked up at the sky and saw the Morning Star. Her heart leaped in her chest. She greeted her eternal friend and said a blessing. At that moment, in spite of her age, or perhaps because of it, Malinalli saw clearly that she had lost nothing, that there was no reason to fear, that the gods were everywhere, not just at her home. Here, too, where she was, a breeze blew, there were flowers, there was song, the Moon and the Morning Star were present, and at dawn the Sun also rose.

With the passing days she confirmed as well that her grandmother had not died. She lived in her thoughts, lived in the cornfields where Malinalli had planted the grains that she brought in her sack. Together, she and her grandmother had chosen the finest grains from the last harvest to be planted before the following rainy season. And although Malinalli could no longer do the sowing with her grandmother's blessings or on her own beloved terrain, it had been a success. The cornfield brimmed with giant ears that were impregnated with the essence of her grandmother and, after the harvest, Malinalli could achieve a kind of communion with her every time she brought a tortilla to her mouth.

⊰⊱

Her grandmother had been her best playmate, her greatest ally, her best friend in spite of the fact that little by little, the years had left her blind. The funny thing was that the less her grandmother was able to see, the less she needed her eyes. She told no one about losing her sight. She got around the same as ever and she knew exactly where everything was. She never stumbled over anything or asked for help. It seemed as if she had sketched out in her mind all the distances, paths, and corners of her surroundings.

When Malinalli turned three, her grandmother gave her clay figurines and toys, a dress she had embroidered when already almost blind, a turquoise necklace, and a small bracelet made of grains of corn. Malinalli felt truly loved. She went out to the patio with her grandmother to play with her new toys. Soon afterward a dark cloud covered them and loud thunder interrupted their games. A bolt of lightning caught Malinalli's attention. It was silver in the sky. What did it mean? What was that silvery splendor on the gray? Before her grandmother could answer her it began to hail. The noise was such that no voice could be heard, only the sound that deafened everything. Malinalli and her grandmother took shelter from the storm inside the house. When the rain stopped, Malinalli asked for permission to go outside and play. Happy and excited, she buried her hands in the ice stones; she erected figures and made circles of ice, till little by little they melted into water. She played for two hours in the mud and water. She soiled her new dress, her knees, and her hands. She made clay dolls and mud balls, and finally she grew tired. When night was already falling, she went back inside the house and said to her grandmother, "Of all the toys that I have been given, I like the toys of water the best."

"Why?" the grandmother asked.

"Because they change shapes."

"Yes, child," the grandmother explained, "they are your

prettiest toys not only because they change shapes, but because they always return, for water is eternal."

The girl felt as if she had been understood and she kissed her grandmother. On receiving the kiss, the grandmother noticed that the child smelled like wet earth and that she was covered in mud from head to toe. It didn't bother the grandmother that Malinalli had soiled her dress or that the child had ruined so quickly what her blind eyes had made with such great effort. On the contrary, she talked to her about the joys of finding pleasure in the water, the earth, and the wind, how giving oneself over to them was a way to relish life.

After the showers, the heat again took hold and gradually it became intolerable. Although it was already night, Malinalli asked for permission to go out and play again and her grandmother, since it was the girl's birthday, let her. The old woman sat by the doorway while her granddaughter laughed and played outside.

After a while, a silence arose. Not another sound was heard. The grandmother grew frightened and went out to look for her granddaughter whom she loved more than her own flesh, than sight itself, than the stars. As she walked, she stumbled upon her and realized that the girl had fallen asleep in the mud. She caressed her with great tenderness, picked her up and carried her into the house. She placed her in her own bed to sleep and remained beside her, watching the stars. She could not see them with her physical eyes but with those of her spirit, eyes with which she had long ago mapped out a planetarium in her heart.

That day the house had been silent and only Malinalli's tiny bell of laughter had filled the spaces and distances of the home. Only the grandmother and Malinalli had celebrated the girl's birthday, for her mother had left a few days before, accompanied by a Tlatoani with whom she had fallen in love, to be in the audience at the ceremony of New Fire, which was celebrated in those parts every fifty-two years. It was an important event, but Malinalli's mother had taken longer than necessary to return. After midnight, laughter and noises were heard coming from Malinalli's mother and her new lord. They returned cheerful and very lively, for the man, by the heat of the New Fire, had proposed and she, very pleased, had immediately accepted. She invited him in and prepared his hammock. When Malinalli's mother was about to lie down to sleep, her mother-in-law interrupted her.

"Three years ago today," she said, "your daughter was born. Today is her birthday. Why weren't you with her? Why didn't you care enough to place the red conch over her pubis?"

"Because then when she is thirteen I would have to perform for her the ceremony of 'rebirth,' and I will not be there to do it."

"How is it that you will not be by her side?"

"I am going to give her away."

"You cannot rip her from me. She belongs to my heart, she belongs to my feelings. In her is the image of my son. Or have you forgotten him?"

"Everything is forgotten in this life," she answered in a cutting tone. "Everything lapses into memory. Every event ceases to be present, loses its value and meaning, everything is forgotten. Now I have a new lord and I will have new children. Malinalli will be given to a new family who will take care of her, for she is a part of the Old Fire that I want to forget.

"No," the grandmother demanded, "I am the one who is here to show her the way, to smooth out her existence, to prove to her that the dream in which we live can be a pleasant one, full of songs and flowers."

"We don't all dream the same thing," the daughter-in-law replied. "The dream can be cruel and sorrowful as mine has been. She will be given away because everything in this life is forgotten."

"It is obvious," the grandmother said in an authoritative voice, "that you will neither shed a tear nor worry over what happens to your daughter. I see that you have forgotten the advice of your mother and father. Do you think that you came to this earth to act wildly, to go to bed and rise merrily with your new lord? Have you forgotten that it was the God of All Things who gave you that girl so that you may show her the way through life? If that's the case, then let me care for her. As long as I live, let Malinalli remain by my side."

Malinalli's mother complied with the grandmother's wishes, and so it was that from that day forward the girl was lovingly educated by her grandmother.

As a result of the long talks between grandmother and granddaughter, from the age of two the girl's speech had been precise, abundant, and well structured. By the time Malinalli was four, she could express doubts and complex concepts without difficulty. The credit was her grandmother's. Very early on, she had taught Malinalli how to sketch out codices in her mind so that she could exercise both language and memory.

"Memory," she told the girl, "is seeing things from the inside. It gives shape and color to words. Without images, there is no memory."

Afterward, she would ask the child to draw on a piece of parchment a codex, a sequence of images that narrate an event. It could be real or made up. The girl spent long hours drawing and at night, the grandmother would ask her to narrate her codex before going to sleep. This is how they played together. The grandmother greatly enjoyed the intelligence and creativity with which her granddaughter elaborated on the images she had made on the parchment.

Malinalli never imagined that her grandmother was blind. She thought her grandmother behaved normally and spoke beautifully. The tone of her grandmother's voice caressed her ears and made her feel an enormous joy. It could even be said that Malinalli was in love with her grandmother's eyes and with the sound of her voice. When the grandmother told a story, Malinalli watched her grandmother's eyes with an unbridled curiosity, for she saw there a beauty that she had not seen in any other person. What most attracted her was that her grandmother's eyes lit up only when she spoke. When the grandmother was silent, her eyes lost all their vivacity, they faded out. It was only by accident that Malinalli discovered that this happened because her grandmother could not see.

One afternoon, when the grandmother was resting in the back of the house, Malinalli, without making a sound, approached her grandmother carrying a small bird cupped in her hands.

"Grandma, see how it suffers?"

"What suffers?" the grandmother asked.

"Can't you see it here in my hands? It's hurt and I want to heal it."

"No, I can't see it. Where is it hurt?"

"One of its wings."

The grandmother reached out her hands and Malinalli put the small bird in them. For Malinalli it was a great surprise to watch her grandmother try to find the bird's injury by touch.

"Citli, how can it be that you who see everything, see nothing? If your eyes don't see colors, don't see my eyes, don't see my face, don't see my codices, what is it that they see?"

"I see what is behind things," the grandmother answered. "I can't see your face, but I know that you are beautiful; I can't see your outside, but I can describe your soul. I have never seen your codices, but I have seen them through your words. I can see all the things that I believe in. I can see why we are here and where we will go when our games end."

Malinalli began to weep silently.

"Why are you crying?" the grandmother said.

"I'm crying because I can see that you do not need your eyes to look or to be happy," she answered. "And I'm crying because I don't want you to go."

The grandmother tenderly took her into her arms. "I will never leave you. Every time that you see a bird in flight, there I'll be. In the form of the trees, there I'll be. In the mountains, the volcanoes, the cornfields, there I'll be. And, above all things, each time that it rains I will be near you. In the rain we will always be together. And don't worry about me, I went blind because I was disturbed at how the appearances of things would confuse me and not allow me to see their essence. I went blind to return to the truth. It was my own decision, and I am happy with what I now see."

The sun had risen. That morning the light was more fluid and the clouds sketched fantastic animals in the sky. Malinalli, accompanied by the memory of her grandmother, stopped her work at the grinding stone to light the fire that would heat the *comal*, the clay dish where the corn flour would become tortillas.

She did this slowly and in reverent silence, for it was to be the last time she would light the fire there. For a moment she watched the shapes of the flames, trying to guess their meanings. The god Huehuetéotl, the Old Fire, showed her his finest shapes and colors. The red and yellow sparks mingled with the green and blue to paint stellar maps in Malinalli's eyes, which put her in a place outside the realm of time. For a moment, she was filled with peace.

In this state, Malinalli shaped the dough with her palms and made two tortillas that she set to cook in the *comal*. She ate the first one slowly, so that she could feel the presence of her grandmother and of the Lord Quetzalcóatl inside her body. The other she let burn completely and later crushed in the grindstone until the tortilla was nothing but a fine ash that she tossed in the air to leave a trace of its presence in that place, so that the wind would speak for her about her past, about her childhood, about her grandmother.

After completing this intimate personal ceremony, Malinalli proceeded to pack her belongings. In a burlap sack she put the necklaces that her grandmother had bequeathed to her, a few grains of corn from her field, plus a few cacao beans, very valuable coins that she could use if the need arose. As she put them in the sack, she yearned to be as precious as a cacao bean, for then she would be highly valued and no one would think of giving her away again.

As soon as she had finished, she washed, dressed, and combed her hair with great care. Before leaving, she blessed the earth that had nourished her, as well as the water, the air, and the fire, asking the gods to be with her, to guide her, to lend her their light so that she might come to know their wishes and commands, in order to be able to fulfill them. She asked their blessing so that anything she might do or say from that moment on would be beneficial to herself, to her people, to the cosmos. She asked the Sun to lend her the strength of its voice so that she might be heard by all; and the Rain to help her fertilize all that she had planted.

She covered with earth the ashes remaining from that which had been her old fire, and left, the weight of fifteen years on her back and the presence of her grandmother and Quetzalcóatl in her gut.

❧✦❧

That day, Cortés had arisen at dawn, restless. The few snatches of sleep he had managed to obtain had been interrupted by dreadful nightmares. The most terrifying was the one that came from a dream that he had had years before, in which he saw himself surrounded by strangers who indulged him with courtesies and honors, treating him like a king. At the time, that dream had filled him with joy and had given him the certainty that he would one day become someone important. However, the night before, the dream had become a nightmare, the honors this time appearing as ridicule, as whispering intrigues, as knives with eyes that fixed themselves on his back . . . as death. The worst of it was that upon opening his eyes, the dream continued, the fear still there, crouching in the darkness. He did not like the dark. It shrunk his soul. During his long sea voyages, he would always look for the North Star in the sky, the sailor's star, so that he would not feel lost. When it was cloudy and he could not see the stars, sailing through a black sea filled him with anxiety.

Not knowing the language of the natives was the same as sailing through a black sea. For him, the Mayans were as inscrutable as the dark side of the moon. Their unintelligible voices made him feel insecure, vulnerable, and he had no trust in his translator. He did not know how faithful Friar Jerónimo de Aguilar was to his words, or how capable he was of betrayal. The friar had arrived practically as if dropped from the heavens. The survivor of a shipwreck years before, Aguilar had been imprisoned by the Mayans. In captivity, he had learned their language and the customs of their culture. Cortés had felt very fortunate when he found out about him and promptly had him rescued. From the very beginning, Aguilar gave Cortés crucial information about the Mayans and, above all, about the extensive and powerful Aztec empire. Aguilar had proved useful as interpreter between Cortés and the natives of the Yucatán, but he had shown little ability to negotiate or persuade since, clearly, had he possessed those skills, the first battles between the Spaniards and the natives would not have been necessary. Cortés preferred to resort to dialogue rather than arms. He fought only when he failed in the field of diplomacy. He soon had no choice.

He had won the first battle. His instinct for victory had led to the defeat of the natives in Cintla. Of course, the presence of horses and artillery had also played a very important role in that, his first triumph on foreign soil. However, far from feeling festive and wanting to celebrate, he was seized by a sense of helplessness.

At an early age he had developed confidence in himself through the ease with which he managed words, interweaving them, applying them, and using them in the most suitable and convincing fashion. Throughout his life as he matured, he confirmed that there was no better weapon than a good speech. Yet now he felt vulnerable and useless, disarmed. How would he be able to use his best and most effective weapon on those natives, who spoke other languages?

Cortés would have given half his life if he could master the languages of that strange country. In Hispaniola and Cuba he had advanced and won positions of power thanks to his speeches, which were embellished with Latin phrases and showed off his knowledge.

Cortés knew that there would not be enough horses, artillery, and harquebuses to achieve dominion over these lands. These natives were civilized, different from those in

Hispaniola and Cuba. Cannons and horses were effective when dealing with savages, but in a civilized context, the ideal thing was to seal alliances, negotiate, win over, and all this could be done only through dialogue, of which he was deprived from the very start.

In this recently discovered world, Cortés knew that he had the opportunity of a lifetime in his hands, yet he felt shackled. He couldn't negotiate and he urgently needed some way to master the language of the natives. He knew that by any other means—sign language, for example—it would be impossible to accomplish his aims. Without the mastery of the language, his weapons were useless; it would be like using a harquebus as a club instead of firing it.

His thoughts came so swiftly that in a matter of seconds he could devise new purposes and new truths that would serve him in maintaining life according to his convenience. But these ideas and goals rested upon the strength of his speeches. He was also convinced that fortune favored the brave, but in this case, courage—which he possessed in abundance—was of little use to him. This was a mission that would be built from the start on the basis of words. Words were its bricks, courage its mortar. Without words, without language, without speeches, there was no mission, and with no mission, no conquest.

The night that had ushered in the new day had filled Montezuma's head with nightmares. The emperor had dreamed of children who were walking naked on the snow that covered the volcanoes of Popocatépetl and Iztaccíhuatl. They did it willingly, even though they would be sacrificed so that Huitzilopochtli would be nourished. Montezuma saw how those children were drowned in a spring and how their bodies floated. Then he saw that the God of Water was walking over them and that fat drops of water fell from the sky, the same as the emperor Montezuma held in his eyes when he awoke. Later, not sleeping, he imagined that the skulls of the children would be the cups from which all of them would drink water. This image caused him to feel at once both fear and pleasure. Perhaps the latter was what most horrified him. Suddenly, a violent wind blasted the door open and let the sunlight fall on Montezuma's face.

His eyes would breakfast on wind and light that morning. The violent gusts shook the curtains, ripped things from their place, and cast objects onto the floor of the room where Montezuma had slept. Horror overcame the leader and his mind fabricated at great speed a series of images of exemplary punishments: agave thorns piercing the tongue, or the penis, bloody needles that spoke of guilt, of the great guilt that Montezuma bore on his shoulders because his people, the Aztecs, had betrayed and distorted the principles of the ancient Toltec religion.

The Aztecs had been a nomadic people until they established themselves in Tula. The mythic founder of Tula was Quetzalcóatl, the Plumed Serpent, and Montezuma was sure that the arrival of the Spanish was due to the fact that Quetzalcóatl had returned and was coming to get his due. Fear of the god's punishment paralyzed his enormous skill for war. Otherwise, he would have wiped out the foreigners in a single day.

THREE

It was the middle of spring when they baptized Malinalli. She was dressed all in white. There was no color on her dress, but a great deal of embroidery. She knew the value of embroidery, of spinning thread and the art of feathers, and had chosen for the occasion a ceremonial *huipil*, full of meaning, that she herself had made.

The *huipiles* spoke. They said much about the women who had made them. They spoke of their time, their social condition, their marital state, their connection to the cosmos. Putting on a *huipil* was a whole initiation; in doing so one repeated daily the voyage from the interior to the exterior. On putting one's head through the opening of the huipil, one moved from the world of dreams, which was revealed in the embroidery, into everyday life, which appears when the head comes out. This awakening to reality is a ritual morning act that reminds us day after day of the significance of birth. *Huipiles* keep one's head centered, with the rest of the body covered in the front, in the back, and on both sides. The cross that is formed by the embroidered parts of the *huipil* means that one is planted in the center of the universe, lit by the Sun and covered by the Four

Winds, the Four Directions, the Four Elements. That's how Malinalli felt in her beautiful white *huipil* as she was ready to be baptized.

For her the ritual of baptism was very important, and she was deeply moved to know that it was the same for the Spaniards. Her ancestors performed it according to their own customs. Her grandmother performed it for her after she was born, and it was assumed that at the age of thirteen it needed to be done for her again, but no one did it. Malinalli very much regretted it.

The number thirteen was very significant. Thirteen were the moons in a solar year. Thirteen menstruations. Thirteen, the houses of the sacred calendar of the Mayans and the Mexicas. Each of its houses was made up of twenty days and the sum of thirteen houses, each with twenty days, came to a total of 260 days. When one was born, both the solar calendar of 365 days and the sacred one of 260 days began and did not join again until the fifty-second year, a complete cycle that would begin again. If you add five and two, the numbers in fifty-two, you get seven, which is also a magic number because seven are the days that make each of the four lunar phases. Malinalli knew that the first seven days, when the moon was between the Earth and the Sun, the Moon is dark, for the new moon is on the verge of rising, and this was a time to be silent so that all things that had yet to be born would do so freely, without any interference. It was the best time to "feel" what should be the main objective of the actions one would undertake during the coming lunar cycle. It was the birth of purpose. The next seven days, when the moon rose at noon and fell at midnight, showing only half her face, was the time to put one's purposes into action. The next seven days, when the Moon was on the opposite side of the Earth from the Sun, and shone in fullness over the earth, was the time to celebrate and share our achievements. And the last seven days, when the Moon showed the other half of her face, was a time to reflect on everything gained over those twenty-eight days.

All these aspects of time accompanied each human being from the moment of birth. Malinalli had been born in the twelfth house. The date of birth marked one's fate and because of this Malinalli bore the name of the house in which she was born. The meaning of the number twelve is resurrection. The glyph that corresponds to the number twelve is a skull in profile, for it represents all that dies and is transformed. Growing out of the skull instead of hair is *malinalli*, a fiber also known as sacred grass. The glyph for twelve alludes to death, which embraces her dead son and offers him rest. It represents either unity or a mother who snatches from death the bundle of a corpse wrapped in its shroud and bound with *malinalli*, the sacred grass. She takes him to return him to the unity of the One and give birth to him, renewed. *Malinalli* was also the symbol of the town, as well as of the bewitching city of Malinalco, founded by the terrestrial-lunar goddess Malínal-Xóchitl, or flower of *malinalli*.

Curiously, it was the fiber *malinalli* that was used to make the poncho which Juan Diego was wearing in the year 1531, when the Virgin of Guadalupe appeared to him supported by the moon, on the twelfth day of the twelfth month, and twelve years after Hernán Cortés had arrived in Mexico.

⋘⋙

Malinalli was so proud of all these concepts contained in the meaning of her name that she tried to give form to them in the *huipil* that she had begun to embroider several moons earlier.

It was during the time of silence that she had felt the

need to make it, and until now she had believed that it was the proper thing to do. The *huipil* was the one that she chose to wear in the longed-for ceremony of baptism. Made with cotton thread that she herself had spun and woven in a loom, it had been appliquéd with seashells and precious feathers. The symbol for the moving wind was embroidered on the chest, surrounded by plumed serpents. It was in itself an encrypted message to be seen and appraised by the emissaries of Lord Quetzalcóatl. She was dressed like a faithful devotee, but no one seemed to notice. The only one who seemed to be dazzled by her attire was a horse that drank from a nearby river and that never took its eyes off her throughout the whole baptismal ceremony. Malinalli did not fail to notice and from then on a loving relationship developed between them.

After the ceremony ended, Malinalli approached Friar Aguilar, to ask him about the meaning of Marina, the name they had just given her. The friar responded that Marina was she who came from the sea.

"Is that all?" Malinalli asked.

The friar responded with a simple, "Yes."

The disappointment must have been evident in her eyes. She was hoping that the name granted to her by the emissaries of Quetzalcóatl would have a deeper meaning since, as she assumed, it wasn't being granted to her by simple mortals who were completely ignorant of the profound meaning of the universe, but by initiates. Her name had to mean something important. She persisted with the friar, but the only additional answer that she could get from him was that they had chosen the name because Malinalli and Marina shared a certain phonetic similarity.

No. She refused to believe it. But because it was such a momentous day in Malinalli's life, she did not let herself sink into disappointment, but instead decided on her own to take control of her new name. If her native name meant braided grass, and if the grass and all plants in general needed water, and her new name was related to the sea, it meant that she was assured of eternal life, for water was eternal and it would forever nourish who she was: the braided grass. Yes, that was exactly the meaning of her new name!

She wanted to pronounce it right away but found it impossible. The "r" in Marina got stuck on the tip of her tongue and the most that she could accomplish, after a few attempts, was to utter "Malina," which left her very frustrated.

One of the things that most amazed her was that with the same oral apparatus, human beings were capable of emitting an infinite amount of different sounds. And she, who considered herself a great imitator, could not understand why she could not pronounce the "r." She asked Aguilar to pronounce her new name, time and again, and she did not take her eyes once from the friar's lips, who patiently repeated "Marina" again and again. It became clear to Malinalli that what was needed to pronounce the "r" was to place her tongue behind her teeth for only a moment, but her tongue, up against her palate as she was used to, could not move quickly enough and the results were disastrous. It was obvious that she would need a lot of practice, but she was not ready to give in.

Ever since she was a girl, she had been able to use her tongue to replicate any sound. When she was one, she had loved to babble, to make noises and little bubbles of saliva with her mouth, to imitate any sound that she heard. She paid great attention to the songs of birds, to the barking of dogs. Surrounded by the silence of the night, she liked to discover distant noises and identify the animal that was emitting this or that sound so that she could later imitate it.

Until the arrival of the Spaniards, her method of learning had been very effective, but the new language had brought to her life new and complicated challenges.

Wanting to try another word so that she would not feel so frustrated, she decided to ask the friar about his god. She wanted to know everything about him: his name, his qualities, how she might approach him, to speak to him, to celebrate him, to worship him. She had loved listening to the sermon before the baptism—which Aguilar himself had translated for them—in which the Spaniards had asked that they no longer be fooled by false gods who demanded human sacrifice. They said that the true god, whom they brought with them, was good and loving and would never demand such a thing. In Malinalli's eyes, that merciful god could be none other than the Lord Quetzalcóatl, who in new garments was returning to these lands to reinstate his kingdom in harmony with the cosmos. She wanted to welcome him, to speak to him.

She asked the friar to teach her how to pronounce the name of their god. Aguilar kindly complied and Malinalli, overcome with emotion, realized that the word, not having any "r"s in it, did not present a problem at all. Malinalli clapped her hands like a young child. She was delighted, thrilled by the sense of belonging that she felt when able to pronounce the name that another social group had assigned to something. It filled her with joy, for nothing disturbed her more than the feeling of being excluded. Right away, Malinalli asked the friar the name of the god's wife. Aguilar told her that he had no wife.

"But then, who is that lady with the child in her arms whom you place in the temple?"

"She is the mother of Christ, of Jesus Christ, who came to save us."

She was a mother! The mother of them all, and so she had to be the lady Tonantzin. It was no coincidence that when the friar had celebrated the mass before the baptism, Malinalli felt enraptured by a feeling that she could not understand. It was a sort of nostalgia for the maternal arms, a longing to feel enveloped, embraced, sustained, and protected by her mother, as at one time she must have been; by her grandmother, as she definitely had been; by Tonantzin, as she hoped she would be; and by a universal mother, like that white lady who held the child in her arms. A mother who wouldn't give her away, who wouldn't let her go, who wouldn't let her fall to the ground but would raise her to the sky, offer her to the four winds, allow her to recover her purity. All these thoughts kept her company as the Spanish priest said Mass in a language that she did not understand, but could imagine.

⊰◦⊱

Like Malinalli, Cortés also thought about his mother, and the countless times she had led him by the hand to church to pray for the health of her sickly child. She was constantly preoccupied with helping overcome his shortness, his physical weakness, and his condition as only child. It was clear that in a society dedicated to the art of war and in which street fights were common, a boy with these characteristics was destined for failure, and perhaps because of this his parents had made sure they provided him with a good education.

During the Mass, Cortés remembered the moment that he had said good-bye to his mother before leaving for the New World. He remembered her tears, her grief, and the portrait of the Virgin of Guadalupe she had given him so that she would always be with him. Cortés was sure that it was the Virgin who had saved his life after the scorpion had bitten him and he asked at that time that she never abandon

47

him, that she watch over him, that she become his ally and help him triumph. He wanted to prove to his mother that he could be more than a simple page in the service of the new king.

He was prepared to do anything. To disobey orders, to fight, to kill. It wasn't enough to have been mayor of Santiago de Cuba. He wasn't troubled over having ignored the instructions of Governor Diego Velázquez, according to which it was recommended not to take risks, to treat the Indians wisely, to gather information about the secrets of that mysterious land, and to find Grijalva, who had led the previous expedition. Cortés had come on a voyage of exploration, not of conquest; with the aim of discovering, not of populating. What Velázquez expected from him was to explore the coastal regions of the gulf and to return to Cuba with some gold as ransom, peacefully obtained; but Cortés was much more ambitious than that.

If his mother could have seen him now—conquering new lands, discovering new places, naming new things. The sense of power that he felt when he gave something or someone a new name must be comparable, he imagined, to that of giving birth. The things that he named were born in that moment and began a new life because of him. The bad part of this was that at times his imagination failed him. Cortés was good at strategizing, forming alliances, conquering, but not at inventing original names. Perhaps that was why he so admired the sonority and musicality of the Mayan and Náhuatl languages. He was incapable of coming up with names like Quiahuiztlan, Otalquiztlan, Tlapacoyan, Iztacamaxtitlan, or Pontonchan, so he searched the Spanish language to name each person and place them under his power in the most conventional way possible. For example, the Totonacan village of Chalchicueyecan he renamed Veracruz, since he had arrived there on the twenty-second day of April 1519, a Good Friday, the day of the True Cross, *la Verdadera Cruz*: hence, Vera Cruz.

The same happened with the Indians that he had just been given. He chose the commonest names for their baptism, not bothering himself much about the matter. However, this didn't prevent him from listening to the Mass before the baptism with great fervor. He was moved by the zeal in the eyes of the natives, despite the fact that the Mass as such was completely new to them. What he didn't realize was that, for the natives, changing the names or the forms of their gods did not pose a problem. Each of their gods was known by at least two different names and appeared to them in different shapes, so the fact that a Spanish Virgin had been placed in the pyramid where before they had worshipped their ancient gods, was something that could be overcome with faith.

Cortés, who had been an altar boy, had never felt a faith so united. And he thought that if these natives, instead of directing their faith toward a false god, would channel it with the same eagerness toward the true god, they were going to be able to produce great miracles. This thought led him to conclude that perhaps it was his true mission to save all the natives from darkness, to put them in touch with the true faith, to end idolatry and the nefarious practice of human sacrifice. In order to accomplish this, he needed to establish power, which could only be gained by challenging the mighty empire of Montezuma. With all the faith he could summon, he prayed to the Virgin to help him triumph in this undertaking.

Cortés was a man of faith. Faith lifted him, gave him stature, transported him beyond time. And precisely at the moment that he most ardently prayed for help, his eyes met Malinalli's, and a maternal spark connected them with the same longing. Malinalli felt that this man could protect her; Cortés, that the woman could help him as only a mother could: unconditionally.

Neither of them knew whence this feeling surged, but as they felt it they accepted it. Perhaps it was the atmosphere of the moment, the incense, the candles, the chants, the prayers, but the fact was that both were transported to their time of greatest innocence, to their childhood.

Malinalli felt as if her heart caught fire from the abundant heat emitted from the candles that the Spaniards had put in the place that had once been a temple dedicated to her ancient gods. She had never seen a candle. Many times she had lit torches and censers, but never a candle. She found it absolutely magical to see so many little fires, so much light reflected, so much illumination coming from such meager flames. She let the fire speak to her from all those minuscule voices and was dazzled by the reflection of the candlelight in Cortés's eyes.

Cortés turned away from her gaze. Faith lifted him, but Malinalli's eyes returned him to reality, to the flesh, to desire, and he did not want the brilliance in her eyes to shatter his plans. He was in the midst of Mass—and an undertaking that he had to respect and to make others respect, including the orders forbidding them from taking for themselves a native woman.

His own attraction to women was, however, uncontrollable and it took great effort to rein in his instincts. So, to avoid temptation he decided to assign that native woman to Alonso Hernández Portocarrero, a nobleman who had accompanied him from Cuba and whom he wanted in his good graces. The gift of an Indian woman would very much flatter him. Malinalli stood out from the other slaves in every way. She walked with assurance, was confident, and radiated elegance.

On hearing of Cortés's decision, Malinalli's heart jumped. It was the sign that she had been waiting for. If Cortés, who was the commander of the foreigners, had ordered her to serve under that gentleman who looked like a respectable Tlatoani, it was because he had seen something in her. Of course, Malinalli would have loved to serve directly under Cortés, the main lord, but she didn't complain. She had made a good impression and, from her experience as a slave, she knew that this was essential in order to lead as dignified an existence as possible.

Portocarrero, for his part, was also pleased at Cortés's decision. Malinalli, that child-woman, was intelligent and beautiful, accustomed to obeying and serving. Her first task was to light the fire to prepare his meal. Malinalli went about it immediately, looking for pieces of torch pine, a wood infused with a resin that was ideal for starting a fire. She made a cross of Quetzalcóatl with them, an essential step in the building of a fire. Then took a good-size dry stick and began to rub it over the torch pine.

Malinalli knew how to bring forth the fire like no one else. She never had problems lighting it, but on this occasion the fire seemed to be annoyed with her. The cross of Quetzalcóatl refused to catch fire. Malinalli asked herself why. Could Lord Quetzalcóatl be upset with her? Why? She had not betrayed him, but rather, had participated in the ceremony of baptism with her mind filled with the memory of him—in fact, even before the ceremony! For she remembered that on entering the temple where the Mass was celebrated, her heart leapt with joy when she saw a cross in the middle of the altar, which for her belonged to the Lord Quetzalcóatl, but that the Spaniards considered as their own. She could not help but be moved. Not for a single moment had she betrayed her beliefs. But the torch pine refused to listen to her, and that was a bad omen.

Distressed, Malinalli began to sweat. To fix the problem, she decided to look for dry grass. To get to the place where it was she had to cross the field where the horses were grazing. Among them, she spotted the one that had been with her at the river during her baptism. Her silent friend, the horse, approached her and for a short while they observed each other. It was a magical moment of mutual admiration and acknowledgment.

Of all of the foreigners' possessions, horses were what had most caught her attention. She had never seen such animals and immediately fell under their powers of seduction. So much so, that the second word that Malinalli learned to say after "God" was "horse."

She loved the horses. They were like gigantic dogs, except that with horses one could manage to see oneself reflected in their eyes. She could perceive no such clarity in the eyes of dogs, much less the dogs that the Spaniards had brought with them. Unlike the *itzcuintlis*, the native dogs, they were aggressive, violent, and cruel looking. The eyes of the horses were kind. Malinalli felt as if the eyes of horses were mirrors where everything you felt was reflected; in other words, they were mirrors into the soul.

She had had her first experience with them on the day that she arrived at the camp. The effect was indescribable. She could not find the words to convey what she felt when she placed her hand on the horse's mane, for the *itzcuintlis* did not have a mane nor were they anywhere near the size of these creatures. But she had learned to love horses even before touching them. She watched from afar, during the battle of Cintla, and became infatuated with them. That day, before the battle, they had ordered the women and children to evacuate the town and to remain a good distance away. But Malinalli's curiosity was more powerful than her will to obey. Some people who had seen the Spaniards mounted on their horses had told her that the foreigners were half beasts, others that the animals were half men and half gods, and others yet, that they were one being. Malinalli decided to find out for herself, and she hid in a place that would allow her to watch the battle without risking her life. At a certain point, one of the Spaniards fell on the ground and she could see how the horse avoided stepping on him at all costs, even though they were in full flight. That same horse was forced by the stampede of other horses to move from its spot and so inevitably its master became entangled underneath. It had no other choice but to step on its master, but the horse did it gingerly, without letting all its weight fall on its hoof so as not to hurt the rider. From that point on, Malinalli felt great admiration for horses. She knew that those animals could cause no harm; their loyalty had been proved. She could trust them, which couldn't be said about every human being.

For example, Cortés's eyes unsettled her. On the one hand she was attracted to them, but on the other they filled her with suspicion. Sometimes his gaze was more like a dog's than a horse's. His very physical appearance was that of a strong, brutish, and savage animal. The thick hair on his arms, chest, and face made this evident. Since the natives' bodies were virtually hairless, she had never seen a man like that until now. She was dying to know what it would be like to caress it, to pass her hand over his chest, his arms, his legs, his crotch; but in her position as a slave, she had to keep her distance. And it was what she preferred. She had already felt Cortés's gaze on her hips and on her chest, and she did not care for it. Cortés's eyes were like the eyes engraved on the flint knives that were used to take out the hearts of sacrifices. They were eyes not to be trusted, for like the eyes in the knives they could plunge themselves into the chest and cut out the heart.

She liked the eyes of her new master Portocarrero better. They were eyes that looked on her indifferently; but since for her indifference was what she knew best, the familiar treatment with which she had always lived, she was happy to be with him. And in order to please him she had to carry out the first task that he had assigned to her. Hastily, she grabbed a handful of dry grass and with it had no problem starting the fire in order to make tortillas for her new master.

Her heart filled with relief. She was building a new fire, in a different way, with a new name and new masters that brought with them new ideas and customs. She was grateful and convinced that she was in good hands and that these new gods had come to end human sacrifices.

❧❦❧

Malinalli, with her new name, recently baptized and purified, would now, at Cortés's side, begin the most important phase of her life. The bonfire was powerful and to give it even more life, Malinalli took a fan to it. The lighting of the fire was an important ceremony. Malinalli remembered with surprising clarity the last time that she had lit a fire in the presence of her grandmother. She was a young girl, and it was early in the morning when her grandmother spoke to her.

"Today I will leave these lands. I will not see the destruction of this world of stone, the writings of stone, the flowers of stone, the cloths of stone that we built as mirrors for the gods. Today the songs of birds will carry my soul into the air, and my lifeless body will stay behind to return to the earth, the mud, and one day it will rise again in the sun that is hidden in the corn. Today, my eyes will open in bloom and I will leave these lands. But before I do, I will sow all my affection in you."

Without warning, a sudden rain began to fall over the region. The grandmother laughed, and with her laughter filled the room with music. Malinalli did not know whether or not her grandmother had been in jest when she spoke of going away some place. The only thing she knew was that her grandmother and she were the same age, that there was no time or distance between them, that she could always play and share her longings, her uncertainties, and her fantasies with her beloved grandmother, who had become a child again. The grandmother asked Malinalli to go out and play in the rain. Thrilled, the girl obeyed. Soon, everything was mud outside the house. They both sat down on the ground and eagerly began to play with the wet earth. They made animal shapes and magical figurines. A kind of madness seemed to possess the grandmother and in a frenzy she shared it with her granddaughter. The grandmother asked the child to cover her eyes with mud, to refresh them with the mud. The child, amused, caressed her grandmother's face trying to comply exactly with the old woman's crazy wishes.

"Life always offers us two possibilities," the grandmother said after she was completely caked in mud, "day and night, the eagle or the serpent, creation or destruction, punishment or mercy, but there is always a third possibility hidden that unites the other two. Find it."

After saying these words, the grandmother raised her mud-covered eyes to the sky.

"Look, my child! The swimmers of the sky!"

Malinalli observed the amazing flight of eagles soaring above them.

"How did you know that they were there if you can't see them?"

"Because it was raining and when it rains, the waters speak to me. The waters tell me the forms of the animals as it caresses them. They tell me how tall and how hard a tree is by the way it sounds on receiving the rain. And they tell me many other things, like the future of each person as it is sketched in the sky by the fish of the air. One has only to interpret it, and mine is very clear: the four winds have given me their signal."

At that moment their surroundings turned orange and a burst of light surrounded the mind of those two females who looked enraptured, transformed, lifted from the severity of this life to float in the lightness of their dreams. The grandmother sang in different dialects and in unintelligible voices as she embraced her granddaughter with nostalgia and eternal affection. After a while, she asked her to go gather as much dry grass as she could find. When the child had fulfilled her command, they went inside the house and built a new fire with the previous day's embers.

"All birds take their shape from fire," the grandmother said as the dry branches burned. "Thought also has its origin in fire. The tongues of flame pronounce words as cold and exact as the fieriest truth that lips can utter. Remember that words can remake the universe. Any time that you feel confused, watch the fire and offer it your mind."

Fascinated, Malinalli watched the thousand shapes hidden in the fire until it had consumed itself.

"Always remember," the grandmother smiled, "that there is no defeat that the fire cannot consume."

The girl looked at her grandmother again and noticed how tears were flowing through the dry earth that covered her eyes. Then the grandmother took a jade necklace and bracelet from the basket where she kept her belongings and, her voice serene as she put them on her granddaughter, she made a final blessing.

"May the earth become one with the soles of your feet

and keep you firm, may it sustain your body when it loses its balance. May the wind cool your ears and offer you at any hour the answers that will heal all that your anguish might invent. May the fire nourish your gaze and purify the victuals that will feed your soul. May the rain be your ally, may it offer you its caresses, cleanse your body and mind of all that does not belong to you."

The girl felt as if her grandmother was saying her good-bye.

"Don't abandon me, Citli," she said in a wounded voice. "Don't leave."

"I already told you that I would never leave you."

And as she hugged her tightly and covered her in kisses, she offered her granddaughter to the sun. She blessed her in the name of the gods and without words said, "May Malinalli be the one who chases fear away. The one who triumphs over fear, makes it disappear, sets it on fire, banishes it, erases it, the one who is never afraid."

Malinalli remained tangled in her grandmother's arms until she felt completely at peace. When she finally separated herself, she noticed that her grandmother was still. She had ceased to belong to time. She had evaporated from her body, and her tongue had returned to silence.

The child understood that it was death and she wept.

❖❖❖

Now, beginning her new life, lighting a new fire amongst her new owners, she felt happy. Until now, everything had been as she had expected. She wanted to believe that the time of tears was behind her. She felt renewed inside. The few days that had passed since she arrived in the Spanish camp had been unforgettable. She had never felt threatened or unsafe. Of course she had not arrived alone, and not just because she had come accompanied by nineteen other women slaves, but because she had come clothed in her past: the familiar, the personal, the cosmic. She wore a jade necklace that had belonged to her grandmother, tiny bells around her ankles, and covering her body a *huipil* that she herself had sewn and embroidered with precious bird feathers symbolizing a stairway to the sky that she would climb in order to be reunited with her grandmother.

FOUR

Malinalli was washing clothes in the river, on the outskirts of the town of Cholula. She was upset. There was too much noise. Far too much. Not just the noise made by her hands when she scrubbed and rinsed the clothes in the water, but the noise inside her head.

Everything around her spoke of this agitation. The river where she washed the clothes charged the place with music through the force of the waters crashing on the stones. Added to this sound was that of the birds, who were as agitated as ever, the frogs, the crickets, the dogs, and the Spaniards themselves, the new inhabitants of this land, who contributed with the clamorous sounds of their armor, their cannons, and their harquebuses. Malinalli needed silence, calm. In the Popol Vuh, the Sacred Book of their elders, it stated that when everything was at silence—in complete calm, in the darkness of night, in the darkness of the light—then would creation arise.

Malinalli needed that silence to create new and resonant words. The right words, the ones that were necessary. Recently she had stopped serving Portocarrero, her lord, because Cortés had named her "The Tongue," the one who translated what he said into the Náhuatl language, and what Montezuma's messengers said, from Náhuatl to Spanish. Although Malinalli had learned Spanish at an extraordinary speed, in no way could it be said that she was completely fluent. Often she had to turn to Aguilar to help her to translate it correctly, so that what she said made sense in the minds of both the Spaniards and the Mexicas.

Being "The Tongue" was an enormous responsibility. She didn't want to make a mistake or misinterpret, and she couldn't see how to prevent it since it was so difficult translating complex ideas from one language to the other. She felt as if each time she uttered a word she journeyed back hundreds of generations. When she said the name of Ometéotl, the creator of the dualities Omecíhuatl and Ometecuhtli, the masculine and feminine principles, she put herself at the beginning of creation. That was the power of the spoken word. But then, how can you contain in a single word the god Ometéotl, he who is without shape, the lord who is not born and does not die; whom water cannot wet, fire cannot burn, wind cannot move, and earth cannot bury? Impossible. The same seemed to happen to Cortés, who couldn't make her understand certain concepts of his religion. Once she asked him what the name of God's wife was.

"God doesn't have a wife," Cortés answered.

"It cannot be."

"Why not?"

"Because without a womb, without darkness, light cannot emerge, life cannot emerge. It is from her greatest depths that Mother Earth creates precious stones, and in the darkness of the womb that gods and humans take their forms. Without a womb there is no god."

Cortés stared intently at Malinalli and saw the light in the abyss of her eyes. It was a moment of intense connection between them, but Cortés directed his eyes somewhere else, abruptly disconnected himself from her, because he was frightened by that sensation of complicity, of belonging, and he immediately tried to cut off the conversation between them, for, aside from everything else, it seemed too strange speaking about religious matters with her, a native in his service.

"What do you know about God! Your gods demand all the blood in the world in order to exist, while our God offers His own to us with each Communion. We drink His blood."

Malinalli did not understand all of the words that Cortés had just uttered. What she wanted to hear, what her brain wanted to interpret, was that the god of the Spaniards was a fluid god, for he was in the blood, in the secret of the flesh, the secret of love; that he was contained in the eternity of the Universe. And she wanted to believe in such a deity.

"So then your god is liquid?" Malinalli asked enthusiastically.

"Liquid?"

"Yes. Didn't you say that he was in the blood that he offered?"

"Yes, woman! But now answer me, do your gods offer you blood?"

"No."

"Aha! Then you shouldn't believe in them."

Malinalli eyes filled with tears as she replied.

"I don't believe that they have to offer blood. I believe in your liquid god, I like that he is a god who is constantly flowing, and that he manifests himself even in my tears. I like that he is stern, strict, and just, that his anger could create or make the universe vanish in one day. But you can't have that without water or a womb. For there to be songs and flowers, there needs to be water; with it, words rise and matter takes on form. There is life that is born without a womb, but it does not remain long on the earth. What is engendered in darkness, however, in the profundity of caves, like precious gems and gold, lasts much longer. They say that there is a place beyond the sea, where there are higher mountains, and there, Mother Earth has plentiful water to fertilize the earth; and here, in my land, we have deep caves and within them, great treasures are produced—"

"Really? What treasures? Where are these caves?"

Malinalli did not want to answer him and said that she did not know. His interruption bothered her. It proved that Cortés was not interested in talking about his religion, or his gods, or his beliefs, or even about her. It was clear that he was only interested in material treasures. She excused herself and went to weep by the river.

This and many other things made it difficult for them to understand each other. Malinalli believed that words colored memory, planting images each time that a thing was named. And as flowers bloomed in the countryside after a rainfall, so that which was planted in the mind bore fruit each time that a word, moistened by saliva, named it. For example, the concept of a true and eternal god, which the Spaniards had proclaimed, in her mind had borne fruit because it had already been planted there by her ancestors. From them she had also learned that things came to exist when you named them, when you moistened them, when you painted them. God breathed through his word, gave life through it, and because of this, because of the labor and grace of the God of All Things, it was possible to paint in the mind of the Spaniards and Mexicas new concepts, new ideas.

Being "The Tongue" was a great spiritual duty, for it meant putting all her being at the service of the gods so that her tongue was part of the resounding system of the divinity, so that her voice would spread through the cosmos the very meaning of existence. But Malinalli did not feel up to the task. Very often, when translating, she let herself be guided by her feelings and then the voice that came out of her mouth was no other than the voice of fear, fear of being unfaithful to the gods, of failure, fear of not being able to bear responsibility. And truthfully, also fear of power, of taking power.

Never before had she felt what it was like to be in charge. She soon found that whoever controls information, whoever controls meaning, acquires power. And she discovered that when she translated, she controlled the situation, and not only that but that words could be weapons. The finest of weapons.

Words were like lightning, swiftly crossing valleys, mountains, seas, bringing needed information as readily to monarchs as to vassals, creating hope or fear, establishing alliances, abolishing enemies, changing the course of events. Words were warriors, be they sacred warriors like the Lord Aguila, or simple mercenaries. As to their divine character, words transformed the empty space in the mouth into the center of Creation, repeating there the same act with which the universe had been made, by uniting the feminine and masculine principles into one.

Malinalli knew that if life was to thrive, and these two principles remain united, she had to position herself in a circular place to safeguard them, to blanket them, since circular forms were what best contained and protected all of creation. Sharp forms, on the other hand, broke things apart, separated them. The mouth, as feminine principle, as empty space, as cavity, was the best place for words to be engendered. And the tongue, as masculine principle, sharp, pointed, phallic, was the one to introduce the created word, that universe of information, into other minds in order to be fertilized.

But what would fertilize it? That was the great unknown. Malinalli was convinced that there were only two possibilities: union or separation, creation or destruction, love or hatred, and that the outcome would be influenced by "The Tongue," that is, by herself. For she had the power with her words to include others in a common purpose, to clothe them, to shelter them. Or she could exclude them, making them into foes, separate beings with irreconcilable ideas; or into solitary beings who were isolated and destitute as she had been in her status as slave, feeling for so many years what it was like to live without a voice, without being taken into account and forbidden to make any decisions on her own.

But that past now seemed very far away. She, the slave who listened to orders in silence, who couldn't look directly into the eyes of men, now had a voice, and the men, staring into her eyes, would wait attentively to hear what her mouth uttered. She, who had so often been given away, who so many times had been gotten rid of, now was needed, valued, as much as if not more than cacao.

Unfortunately, this privileged position was unstable and could change at any moment. Even her life was in danger. Only a victory by the Spaniards would guarantee her freedom, for reasons that she had not been afraid to state on various occasions in veiled language, that the Spaniards truly had been sent by the Lord Quetzalcóatl, and not only that, but that Cortés himself was the incarnation of the revered god.

Now it was she who could decide what was said and what went unsaid, what to confirm and what to deny, what would be made known and what kept secret. It was a grave dilemma, for it wasn't simply a matter of saying or not saying, or substituting one name for another, but that in doing so she ran the risk of changing the meaning of things. When translating, she could change what things meant and impose her own vision on events, and by doing so enter into direct competition with the gods, which horrified her. Because of her insolence, the gods could very well become annoyed with her and mete out their punishment, and this absolutely frightened her. She could avoid this fate by translating everything as closely to the meaning of the words as possible. But if the Mexicas were to question for a moment—as she herself had—whether or not the Spaniards had been sent by Quetzalcóatl, she would be destroyed along with them in the blink of an eye. So she found herself in a delicate position. Either she remained faithful to the gods and to the meaning that they had given to the world, or she followed her instincts, her most earthly and primary instincts, and made sure that each word and each action acquired the meaning that most suited her. The second choice was clearly a rebellion against the gods, and their eventual reaction filled her with fear and guilt, but she saw no other alternative.

⊷⊱⊰⊶

Malinalli's feelings of fear and guilt were at the least as powerful as those of Montezuma. Weeping, trembling, filled with dread, he awaited the punishment of the gods for how the Mexicas had destroyed Tula long before and in that sacred place dedicated to Quetzalcóatl, had engaged in human sacrifice. Before, in the Toltecan Tula, there had been no need for such practices. It was enough that Quetzalcóatl lit the new fire and accompanied the sun on its path through the celestial dome to maintain balance in the cosmos. Before the Mexicas, the Sun did not feed on human blood; it did not ask for it, did not demand it.

The great guilt that Montezuma bore on his shoulders made him certain that not only was it time to pay old debts but that the arrival of the Spaniards signaled the end of his empire. Malinalli could prevent this from happening. She could proclaim that the Spaniards had not been sent by Quetzalcóatl, and they would be destroyed in a moment . . . along with her, and she did not want to die a slave. She yearned to live in freedom, no longer to be given from one to another, no longer to lead such an errant life.

There was no going back, no way to come out unharmed. She knew too well Montezuma's cruelty, and she knew that if the Spanish were defeated in their venture, she would be condemned to death. Faced with this possibility, she understandably wanted the Spanish to triumph. And if to assure their victory she had to keep alive the idea that they were gods come from the sea, she would do so, although by now she wasn't very convinced of the idea. The hope that one day she would be able to do whatever she wanted, marry whom she wanted, and have children without the fear that they might be taken into slavery or destined as sacrifices, was enough to make her take a step back. What she most wanted was a piece of earth that belonged to her and where she could plant her grains of corn, the ones that she always carried with her and that had come from her grandmother's cornfield. If the Spaniards could make sure that her dreams would crystallize, then it was worthwhile helping them.

Of course, this didn't assuage her guilt or make clear to her what she should say and what she should keep silent about. What kind of a life is worth defending with lies? And who could confirm that they were lies? Perhaps she was being too harsh. Perhaps the Spaniards had been sent by Quetzalcóatl and it was her duty to collaborate with them until she died, sharing with them privileged information that had come directly from the mouth of a woman in Cholula. This woman had loved Malinalli's confident personality, her beauty, and her physical strength, and she wanted her as a wife for her son. With the intent of saving Malinalli's life she had confided in her, warning her that in Cholula they were preparing an ambush against the Spanish. The plan was to arrest them, wrap them up in hammocks, and take them to Tenochtitlán alive. The woman suggested that Malinalli leave the city before this happened and that afterward she could marry her son.

Malinalli now had the burden of deciding whether or not to share this information with the Spaniards. Cholula was a sacred place. One of Quetzalcóatl's temples was situated there. The defense or attack of Cholula meant the defense or attack of Quetzalcóatl. Malinalli was more confused than ever. The only thing she was sure of was that she needed silence to clear her mind.

She implored the gods for silence. What most tormented her, aside from the external noises, were the noises within, the voices in her mind that told her not to say anything, not to give the Spaniards any valuable information that might save their lives, for something was wrong. Perhaps the foreigners were not who she thought they were, not the envoys of Quetzalcóatl. Certainly their recent behavior did not conform to the ideal model that she had devised. She felt disillusioned.

For one thing, there was a total incongruity between the meaning of the name Cortés (courteous) and the man himself. To be *cortés* was to be sensitive and respectful, and she didn't think the man possessed either of these attributes, nor did the men that he had brought with him. She couldn't believe that god's emissaries would behave in such a manner, that they would be so rough, so rude, so ill spoken, even insulting their own god when they were angry. Compared to the gentleness and lyricism of the Náhuatl, Spanish was a bit aggressive.

There was one thing, though, that was worse than the unpleasant manner with which the Spanish gave orders, and that was the odor that emanated from them. She never expected that the emissaries of Quetzalcóatl would smell so bad. Cleanliness was common practice among the natives. The Spaniards, on the other hand, did not bathe, their clothes reeked, and neither water nor the sun could rid them of their stench. No matter how much she scrubbed and scrubbed the clothes in the river, she wasn't able to wash from them the smell of rotted iron, of metallic sweat, of rusted armor.

Moreover, the interest that the Spanish and Cortés in particular expressed for gold did not seem right to her. If they in fact were gods, they would be concerned with the earth, with the planting, with making sure that men were nourished, but that was not the case. Never had she seen them interested in the cornfields, only in eating. Hadn't Quetzalcóatl stolen the grain of corn from the Mount of Our Sustenance to give it to mankind? Didn't the Spanish care how the gift had affected men? Weren't they curious to know whether or not they were reminded of its divine origin when they ate it? Whether or not they protected it and venerated it as something sacred? Did they care about what would happen if man stopped planting it? Didn't they know that if man stopped planting corn, it would die out? That the ear of corn needs man's intervention to strip it of the leaves that cover it, so that the seed may be free to reproduce? That there is no way for corn to live without man, nor man to live without corn? The fact that corn needed man to reproduce was proof that it was a gift from the gods to mankind, for without mankind there would have been no need for the gods to give away corn, and mankind, on the other hand, would not have been able to survive on the earth without corn. Didn't the Spaniards know that we are the earth, from earth we were born, that the earth consumes us, and when the earth comes to its end, when the earth is exhausted, when corn no longer sprouts, when Mother Earth no longer opens her heart, it will be our end as well? Then what was the point of accumulating gold without corn? How was it possible that the first word Cortés learned in Náhuatl was precisely the one for gold and not corn?

Gold, known as *teocuitlatl*, was considered to be the excrement of the gods, waste matter and nothing else, so she didn't understand the desire to accumulate it. She thought that when the day came that the grain of corn was not revered and valued as something sacred, human beings would be in grave danger. And if she—who was a mere mortal—knew this, how was it possible that the emissaries of Quetzalcóatl, who came in his name, though under a different guise, who communicated with him, did not know it? Was it possible that these men were more likely emissaries of Tezcatlipoca than Quetzalcóatl?

Quetzalcóatl's brother had once deceived him with a black mirror, and that is what it seemed the Spaniards were doing with the natives, but this time with resplendent mirrors. Tezcatlipoca, the god who sought to overthrow his brother, was a magician. Showing off his talents, he sent a black mirror to Quetzalcóatl in which Quetzalcóatl saw the mask of his false holiness, his dark side. In response to such a vision, Quetzalcóatl got so drunk that he even fornicated with his own sister. Full of shame, the following day he left Tula to find himself again, to recover his light, promising to return one day.

The great mystery was whether indeed he had returned or not. What was most troubling for Malinalli, independent of whether or not the Spaniards achieved victory over Montezuma, was that her life and liberty were at risk. All this had begun months earlier, when Cortés had accidentally found out that she spoke Náhuatl. Since Aguilar—who in all the years that they had spent in these lands had only learned Mayan—couldn't help Cortés in understanding Montezuma's messengers, Cortés asked Malinalli to help him translate and in exchange he would grant her her liberty. From that moment on, events followed one after another with extraordinary speed, and now Malinalli found herself trapped in a whirlpool that allowed no escape. Images of moments that had sealed her destiny, going back to the days when the Spaniards had first landed, appeared and disappeared in her mind.

Foremost was the day when the chief of Tabasco had gathered her along with the nineteen other women to tell them that they would be given away as spoils of war to those who had recently arrived, since the foreigners had battled and defeated the people of Cintla.

She remembered in detail the conversation that had taken place among the women on the journey to the Spanish camp. Almost in secret they mentioned the possibility that there might be a connection between the men that arrived from the sea and Quetzalcóatl. The current year was a One Sugarcane year which, according to the Mexica calendar, was the year of Quetzalcóatl, who had been born during a One Sugarcane year and died after a cycle of fifty-two years, also a One Sugarcane. It was said that the coincidence of the Spaniards having arrived during a One Sugarcane year was too powerful to ignore. One of the women said that she had heard that One Sugarcane years were disastrous for kings. If something bad happened during a One Lizard year, the evil befell men, women, and the old. If it happened during a One Jaguar, One Deer, or One Flower year, it befell children, but if it happened during a One Sugarcane year, it befell kings. This had been made evident by the fact that the foreigners had battled triumphantly against the citizens of Cintla and would likewise triumph if they confronted Montezuma. This was a sign that they had come to conquer and to reinstate the kingdom of Quetzalcóatl. And so Malinalli accepted it in her heart; on listening to these words, she was filled with joy and hope and illusion, with a longing for change. To know that the kingdom that permitted human sacrifices and slavery was in peril made her feel at peace with herself.

Far from there, in the palace of Montezuma, the same conversation had taken place but between Montezuma, his brother Cuitláhuac and his cousin Cuauhtémoc. Cuitláhuac and Cuauhtémoc thought that Cortés and his men, rather than gods arrived from the sea, were a simple band of plunderers. Montezuma, on the other hand, decided that whether or not they were gods, he would give them preferential treatment, since it was considered that even plunderers were protected by Quetzalcóatl. So he sent off his principal envoy with the following message: "Go with haste, make reverence to our lord, saying that his deputy Montezuma has sent you in honor of their arrival."

Maybe Montezuma was not aware of the great uncertainty that his actions caused among his people, for when they heard that the emperor himself had paid respect to the foreigners, and not just that, but that he put himself at their service, they saw themselves obliged to behave likewise. The preferential treatment toward the Spaniards signified to everyone that the Spaniards were superior to the emperor Montezuma.

But in the light of certain recent events, Malinalli was no longer sure this was so. From the first instance that he had made contact with the messengers from Montezuma, Cortés betrayed his insatiable desire for gold. He wasn't impressed by the feathered arts, or the beauty of the cloths and jewels with which they paid him respect, but with gold. Cortés had forbid the members of his party from trading gold privately, and he set up a table near the camp so that the natives made their trades officially. Every day Totonacans as well as Mexicas came with offers of gold for Cortés that he traded through his servants for pieces of glass and mirrors, for needles and scissors.

Malinalli herself was given a necklace made with pieces of glass and mirror. She very much liked the reflections it produced. She understood mirrors well. When she washed clothes in the river she examined herself in the water and her reflected image spoke to her of fear. She did not like seeing it, for it bothered her, sickened her. She remembered that once as a girl, when she was ill, they had made her watch her image reflected in a pail of water and she had gotten better. She asked the river to speak to her, to heal her, to tell her if she was doing the proper thing, whether or not she was making a mistake. She knew the waters spoke in all receptacles. Her grandmother had told her that in the Anáhuac region there was an enormous visionary lake, where images of what was to come were reflected on the waters, and in that place the holy men had seen an eagle devouring a serpent. The river where she was washing the clothes, however, did not speak to her, said nothing to her, and she could see nothing in it but the filth from the clothes of the Spaniards arrived from the sea.

The sea was a vast expanse of reflections. The lakes and the rivers, as well. In them were contained the sun and the god of the waters. Malinalli knew that she could find something of herself behind each reflection, like the sun reflected in the moon, as well as in the waters, on the stones, in the eyes of others. When using resplendent stones or objects, one is reflected in the cosmos as in a game of mirrors. The sun doesn't realize that it shines, for it cannot see itself. It would have to see itself reflected in order to understand its greatness. That is why we need mirrors, to understand ourselves. That is why Tula, Quetzalcóatl's city, was created to be a mirror of the sky, and that is why Malinalli liked to use shiny objects as mirrors where Quetzalcóatl could be amply reflected. Her necklaces were her most beautiful mirrors.

Taking from her sack the necklace that Cortés had given her, she fastened it around her neck with the intention of being seen by the god. Of meeting him in the reflections. She looked at herself again in the river, and this time the water revealed to her a series of small images, one after the other, in an undulating line. Immediately, it reminded her of the silvery snake that the Spanish soldiers made when they marched one behind the other, the sun reflecting off their armor. She also connected it to the soldiers of Tula, who marched one behind the other, seeing their reflection in the mirror that the one before them carried on his back.

⊷⬥⬦⬥⊶

Although Malinalli wasn't aware of it, Hernán Cortés was only a few steps away from her. Taking advantage of the clear day, he had decided to rest for a moment near the river. A while earlier, he had left off drawing wheels of fortune in his notebooks. Whenever he wanted to relax and clear his mind he would begin drawing wheels of fortune.

Doing so, he would enter a state of deep relaxation, pleased by the concept of a circular time that would cause one to be at the bottom one moment and then, just like that, at the top. But that day a new idea came into his mind and forced him to put aside pen and paper. On drawing the part of the wheel hitting the bottom, he felt as if that moment was the most important in the endless process of the turning: the moment that the wheel spins around to the bottom, that instant of bonding with the earth, all the rest is in the air, floating, where neither the future nor the present exist. This new understanding made him lift his eyes and regard his surroundings with fresh eyes.

Immediately he was in a much more agreeable mood. These new lands, which until now had seemed so strange, so dangerous and inhospitable, where the heat and the giant flies, the humidity and the poisonous plants, had terrorized his heart, suddenly changed their appearance, and he found all his surroundings warm and friendly. He felt as if this land was his, that it belonged to him and that, rather than having voyaged there, he had always been there. With great peace in his heart—something foreign to him—he decided to take a swim in the river. When he got to the shore, he discovered that Malinalli was doing the same thing. She had shed her lovely *huipil* in order to go in.

Cortés caught sight of her naked body, observing her back, her hips, her thighs, and her hair, and was aroused as never before.

Feeling his presence, Malinalli turned, and then Cortés could see her adolescent breasts, firm, enormous, the nipples prominent and pointing directly at his heart. He felt a magnificent erection and with it a huge longing to possess her, but knew he shouldn't, so he waded waist deep into the cold water to see if it would cool his erection a bit. As he approached her, he tried to begin a conversation that would distract him from his thoughts.

"What are you doing?"

"Immersing myself in the god Tláloc, the God of Water."

In the water, facing each other, Cortés and Malinalli looked into each other's eyes and found their destiny and their inevitable union. Cortés understood that Malinalli was his true conquest, that there, in the depths of her black eyes, were the gems he had been searching for all this time. Malinalli, for her part, felt that on Cortés's lips, in his saliva, there was a taste of the divine, a piece of eternity, and she wanted to savor it and guard it with her lips. The clouds in the sky began to move with extraordinary swiftness. The air became laden with humidity, moistening the feathers of birds and the leaves of trees, as well as Malinalli's vagina. The gray clouds, like Cortés's member, made a great effort to contain their waters, to hold back, not to let them fall, so that their precious liquid would not be released. Cortés barely had time to ask, before throwing himself on her, "And what is that god?"

Malinalli still had time to respond before being taken.

"Eternal, the same as yours, but his eternity is not invisible like yours. Our god evaporates, makes designs in the sky, moves whimsically through the clouds, shouts out his presence, spills his consciousness, and quenches our thirst and our fear."

Cortés, his eyes burning with longing, put his hand on Malinalli's breast, interrupting her. "Are you afraid?"

Malinalli shook her head. Cortés then caressed her slowly with his wet hand. He took hold of the girl-woman's nipple with his fingertips. Malinalli trembled. Cortés ordered her to continue speaking about her god. He thought that he would assuage his desire a little, but nothing more. He did not want to break the pact, that all men who were part of this undertaking would respect the native women. Malinalli continued with her speech as best she could, for Cortés had already put her nipple in his mouth and passed his tongue over it lustfully.

"Our god gives us eternal life. . . . That is why our god is water. Hidden in the water, in its invisible parts, is the truth, but we do not come to know it unless we weep or die forever."

Cortés's ambitious mind could not stand it any longer, and he wanted to possess Malinalli and her god at the same time. In his head there was an explosion of pleasure, and the fire of his heart wanted to evaporate forever that god called Tláloc, that god of water. He lifted Malinalli out of the water and carried her to the shore, where he forcefully penetrated her. At that moment, the sky also exploded and let its rain fall over them.

Cortés did not notice the lightning. The only thing that he was aware of was the warmth at the core of Malinalli's body and the way that his member pushed and opened the tight walls of the girl's vagina. He did not care if his passion and force hurt Malinalli. He did not care if lightning struck nearby. All he cared about was going in and out of that body.

Malinalli remained silent and her black eyes, more beautiful than ever, became watery, holding in tears. With each thrust, Malinalli felt the pleasure of Cortés's naked, hairy torso brushing up against her breasts. This was her answer to her uncertainty regarding what she would feel when she touched hairy skin. In spite of the violence done to her body, in her delirium Malinalli remembered what her grandmother had told her in such a sweet voice—as if the

birds, all of them, had imparted their spirits in her throat—
on the day before her death.

"There are tears that are the healing and blessing from
the Lord of All Things. For water is also a language whose
liquid voice sings at the breaking of the light; it is the essence
of our god who brings together extremes and reconciles the
irreconcilable."

For a few minutes—which seemed an eternity—Cortés
penetrated her time and again, like a savage, as if all the
power of nature were contained in his being. Meanwhile,
it was raining so hard that his passion and his orgasm were
drowned in the rains, as were Malinalli's tears. She had for
the time being ceased to be "The Tongue" to become simply
a woman, silent, voiceless, a mere woman who did not bear
on her shoulders the enormous responsibility of building the
conquest with her words. A woman who, contrary to what
would be expected, felt relief in reclaiming her condition
of submission, for it was a much more familiar sensation to
be an object at the service of men than to be a creator of
destiny.

It seemed as if no one else but god had been witness
to that outburst of lustful anger, of passionate vengeance,
of loving hate, but this wasn't so. Jaramillo, a captain in
Cortés's army, had seen them. And the figure of Malinalli
became engraved in his consciousness and he was attracted,
as never before, to this woman whom Cortés, his chief, had
possessed.

FIVE

Malinalli and Cortés entered the bathhouse naked. It was surprising to see Cortés free of his garments and appearances. He seemed smaller and vulnerable. The only requisite condition to fulfill that ritual of purification and rebirth was nakedness. For the cleansing of the blood to take place, it was necessary that all the pores of the body expand, open, and in doing so allow the steam, that other image of water, the spirit of water, to purify the body four times, which corresponded to the four cardinal points, the four stations, the four elements.

It was Cortés's first experience with this sacred practice, which he agreed to participate in at the request of Malinalli. So convinced was she that the gods returned to us our consciences when their essence materialized in the water that she had asked Cortés to relax for a while in the waters before he took any action against the inhabitants of Cholula.

Cortés resisted at first, thinking that the invitation seemed suspicious. What kind of proposition was this, to go into a small circular enclosure that had only one exit, the same as the entrance, and to do so naked and unarmed? The atmosphere in Cholula did not inspire him to have blind faith in anyone. Up to that moment, neither of the two councilors had wanted to receive him. Cholula relied on a worldly councilor, Tlaquiach—lord of the here and now—and a spiritual one, Tlachiac—lord of the world beneath the earth. Both of them lived in houses adjacent to the temple of Quetzalcóatl. The people in Cholula spoke Náhuatl, the language of the empire, and they were subjects of the Mexicas, to whom they paid tribute. But Cholula was an independent dominion and, like Tlaxcala, had a government ruled by various lords. They were a proud people and could not imagine any situation in which their god Quetzalcóatl would fail to protect them, so they did not seem all that fearful of the foreigners. They had plenty of faith in their tutelary god.

Cortés and his men had arrived in Cholula on the way to Tenochtitlán, accompanied by their allies, the Totonacans from Cempoala and the Tlaxcaltecans. The Spaniards entered Cholula after marching the distance of forty kilometers that separated Tlaxcala from Cholula. They were welcomed and fed, but not so the Totonacans and the Tlaxcaltecans, who remained on the outskirts of the city. Only a few hundred went in with the Spaniards, transporting their artillery and other equipment. The reason for this was that the inhabitants of Cholula had old feuds with those of Tlaxcala and in no way would allow them into the city, much less armed.

Cortés was impressed with the beauty and grandness of Cholula. Cholula was a densely populated and prosperous city. Its temples made evident that the city was without doubt one of the most important religious centers of the New World. The main temple, dedicated to the cult of Quetzalcóatl, was the tallest pyramid in Mexico, with 120 steps. Aside from this temple, Cortés counted over four hundred thirty towers, or pyramids, which he called *mezquitas*, or little mosques.

Cholula had some two hundred thousand inhabitants and some fifty thousand houses. It was the most important city that the Spaniards had seen on their long journey inland from the coast. One of its attractions was a huge market whose specialties included feathered works of art, ceramic plates, and precious stones.

But three days after their arrival, the people of Cholula, under the pretext of a shortage of provisions, stopped giving food to the Spaniards, supplying them only with firewood and water. Cortés then had to ask the Tlaxcaltecans to find them food.

There was an atmosphere of suspicion and anxiety permeating the city. Cortés found out from the Tlaxcaltecans that outside the city, troops of Mexicas were gathering. His informants warned him that they were most likely preparing—with the Cholutelcans—an attack on the Spaniards.

Faced with such a climate of intrigue, Cortés had to make a decision. He had already confronted and defeated the Totonacans and Tlaxcaltecans, and had their support, so he had to continue with his plans of conquest. He had to reach Tenochtitlán. He wasn't going to allow them to stop him. He had to make a fateful decision. He, Cortés, was not a mere soldier, he was the emissary and representative of the King of Spain, and the ambush they were preparing against him, by extension, was an ambush directed against the King of Spain. So he had to act in the name of the crown, defending it resolutely and punishing with death the treason that was being hatched against the King of Spain.

Taking these facts into account, it was logical that Cortés had no wish to enter the bathhouse. He was more concerned with attacking before being attacked, than in participating in some kind of pagan ritual. However, Cortés, who never took more than three steps without a bodyguard protecting him, unexpectedly agreed to go into the bathhouse, where he would be literally a prisoner. The reason for his decision was that Malinalli had explained to him briefly that years before, the Toltecans had overthrown the Omelcans, the ancient inhabitants of Cholula, and in that place had established the cult of Quetzalcóatl, a deity who was associated with Venus, the Morning Star, and who accompanied the sun in its trajectory. Quetzalcóatl was a man who had become a god, a god who did not need human sacrifices, did not ask for them, who only needed to set fire with his cane to the old sun so that the new sun rose without any human sacrifices along the way, sacrifices that the Aztecs established when they settled in Tula, betraying the principles of Quetzalcóatl. That is why the Aztecs feared his return—they felt guilty and awaited their punishment.

"If you enter the bathhouse, if you shed all your garments, your metals, shed all your fears and sit on the Mother Earth, near the fire, near the water, you will have the power to be renewed, reborn, elevated, to travel with the wind like Quetzalcóatl, leaving your flesh behind, your human clothing, and transforming yourself into a god. And only a god can defeat the Mexicas."

Cortés forgot his doubts. He had realized the great spirituality of the native people and his warrior's instinct told him that it was the right thing to do. If he could reveal himself to them as their god Quetzalcóatl, no human power could defeat him. And so he assigned two of his captains to guard the entrance to the bathhouse and ordered soldiers to line its perimeter.

Inside the bathhouse, the air was extraordinary. In spite of the semidarkness, you could make out the faces of Malinalli and Cortés in detail, sketched by the tenuous light that entered from the only small opening in that stone womb, that tiny space permeated with hot vapor. Malinalli's good intentions, of putting Cortés in touch with that part of nature responsible for interweaving the perception of the invisible—that which commingles seed with tree, fruit with taste, bark with mud, stone with fire, sperm with thought, thought with stars, stars with pores of the skin, and pores of the skin with the saliva that pronounced the words that expand the universe—were about to come to naught, for the darkness and their nakedness awoke in them an unexpected desire such as they had never felt before.

For Malinalli, the nearness of a man who did not belong to her world or to her race, but who was already a part of her past, made her uneasy. Her memory sharpened and filled her thoughts like needles, reminding her of the pain she felt on being forcefully taken by Cortés. Her body still hurt, but yet, she felt a restlessness, a fervor, a longing to be embraced, touched, and kissed anew.

Cortés, for his part, remembered with his lips the pleasurable sensation of licking and sucking that woman's nipples, and he was overcome by an uncontrollable urge to drink the sweat that dripped from them. But neither of them did anything. They remained still and in total silence.

The air became charged with electricity. Cortés had chosen to sit facing the entrance of the bathhouse, with his back to the adobe wall. This way he could be in control in the event that an enemy entered the intimate enclosure. Malinalli, seated facing him, also sought protection in her own way. She wrapped her arms around her legs, so as to seal the entrance to her body, to her most sensitive part, from the gaze and reach of Cortés.

For Cortés, being in that small space transported him to another time. It made him forget his unquenchable thirst for conquest, his irrepressible desire for power. At that moment, the only thing he wanted was to bury himself between Malinalli's luxuriant legs, so as to drown in the sea of her womb and silence his mind for a moment. That immense longing, that intense need to merge with Malinalli, scared him, for he felt as if he could lose control and give himself for the first time to someone else. He was terrified to lose himself in her and forget the purpose of his life. So instead of taking her, he broke the annoying silence.

"Why are there so many sculptures of snakes? Do they all represent Quetzalcóatl?"

Cortés had seen many stone snakes in Cholula, which frightened and fascinated him with their stares.

"Yes," Malinalli responded.

She didn't want to talk. She wanted to be silent and she wanted Cortés to do the same. She liked him like that, with his mouth closed. When he didn't express himself verbally, Malinalli could imagine that the flower and the song invaded his thought, but when he talked, everything he said contradicted the things that she thought about him, what she yearned for, what she dreamed about. He was definitely more attractive when he was quiet. But Cortés was uncomfortable with silence; he didn't know what to do in that atmosphere of peace. The only thing that occurred to him was to throw himself on Malinalli and take her, but the heat was so intense that he didn't feel like moving.

"And this Quetzalcóatl, as you call him," he persisted, "what kind of god is he? You must know that we were cast out of paradise because of a serpent."

"I don't know what kind of serpent you are talking about. Ours is the image of Quetzal: bird, flight, feather, and Cóatl: serpent. The feathered serpent signifies Quetzalcóatl. The union of rainwater with earth water also signifies Quetzalcóatl. The serpent represents the rivers; the birds, the clouds. The bird serpent and the winged reptile are Quetzalcóatl. The sky below and the earth above are as well."

Then suddenly, without warning, the darkness inside the bathhouse, the stone womb, changed to brightness, as if the word Quetzalcóatl had created the light. Cortés, who understood nothing of the religious beliefs of the inhabitants of those lands, on first hearing this explanation of the god's symbolism, envisioned it as an elegant and majestic image, which definitely united the irreconcilable concepts of that which flies with that which slithers.

Malinalli and Cortés looked into each other's eyes. Silence reigned anew. The gaze of one penetrated the other and, immersed in that intimate space, they both experienced a memory of something that already lived in another part of time. The trembling Cortés felt in the center of his pupils made him cast his look away from Malinalli's infinite black eyes, which in the same moment reflected sorrow, love, and a certain yearning for vengeance.

"And what good has that feathered serpent done to be such an important god?" Cortés demanded. "Because in the ugly manner in which you depict him, he seems more like a devil than a god."

Malinalli, who well knew that the only way to keep Cortés quiet was not to give him a chance to talk, interrupted him, brimming with passion, and responded:

"At first," she said, "mankind was scattered throughout the universe. We were dust that floated where the wind is nothing, where water is nothing, where fire is nothing, where nothing is earth, where scattered mankind is nothing, where nothing is nothing. Quetzalcóatl united us, gave us form, made us. From the stars he made our eyes. From the silence of his being he brought forth our understanding and blew it in our ear. From the sun he ripped an idea and made food for our sustenance, which we call corn, and which is mirror to the sun and has the color that gives life to blood and to our cheeks. Quetzalcóatl is god and our minds are united with his."

Malinalli handed Cortés a receptacle of water with the petals of various flowers and grasses so that he could refresh himself and cool his body, and then she continued.

"Quetzalcóatl was also a wise man, a priest, supreme governor of Tollan."

Malinalli paused to pour some water over the hot stones, which produced even hotter and more penetrating steam and a sound delightful to the ears. But Cortés wanted to know more about Quetzalcóatl. He was thinking of using all the information that he obtained from this conversation for his own personal objectives of conquest.

"What kind of government did he have?" he asked with great curiosity.

"During Quetzalcóatl's regime Tollan was swollen with greatness: jade, coral, and turquoise adorned the world; yellow and white metals, precious metals; seashells, cousins to the ear, spirals of sound, receptacles of song; quetzal feathers, yellow and crimson feathers colored that greatness. There were all kinds of cacao, all kinds of cotton in all colors. Quetzalcóatl was a great artist and a provider of abundance in all his creations. Quetzalcóatl, the Toltec, is he who looks for himself."

"And what happened to him?" Cortés asked.

"At a certain point in his life he stopped searching for himself in everything that exists and gave in to temptations. Or, as you would say, he sinned and later fled."

"Did he steal? Did he murder?" Cortés asked, more interested by the moment.

"No, he was deceived by a sorcerer who changed his destiny. It was Tezcatlipoca, a sorcerer, his brother and the shadow to his light, who one day put a black, deceitful mirror before his eyes, and when Quetzalcóatl looked into it, he saw a deformed face, with giant ears and sunken eyes. He saw the mask of his false identity, his dark side, and he was disturbed by the reflection and frightened by his own face. Right afterward he was invited to drink pulque, which made him intoxicated and frenzied. While drunk, he asked for his sister Quetzalpetatl to be brought before him and with her he drank more still. Completely inebriated, the siblings were overcome with desire, and it was then that they lay down together, driving each other crazy with caresses, making their bodies madly collide with each other, touching and kissing each other till they fell asleep. At dawn, when Quetzalcóatl had regained his consciousness, he wept and set off for the east—toward the place where you arrived—and boarded a raft made of serpents. He went to the black and red land of Tollan, to find himself again, and afterward set himself on fire."

By chance, just at that moment a drop of Cortés's sweat slid past the exact spot where he had been bitten by the scorpion, and he remembered the hallucination of the serpent. He felt thirsty and asked if he could have some water. Malinalli told him that they would give it to him as soon as he went outside.

"Will we be here much longer?"

"No."

"Well then, finish your story," he said.

Their bodies seemed to have become all sweat and pureness by the time Malinalli concluded the story.

"When Quetzalcóatl set fire to himself, a blue spark came from his heart. His heart, all of his being, freed itself from the fire, rose toward the sky, and was transformed into the Morning Star."

With these words, Malinalli ended the ritual of the bathhouse and invited Cortés to leave that womb. Malinalli was relieved, knowing full well that water cleanses everything, softens everything. If it was capable of polishing stones in a river, what then could it not do inside the human body? Water could utterly purify and brighten even the hardest of hearts. Although Malinalli had not been able to pray to the God of Water as was her custom inside the bathhouse, since Cortés had done nothing but interrupt her, she felt in some way that the ritual had been effective. She watched Cortés emerge from the bathhouse purified, reborn, changed. Like a serpent, he had shed his old skin; he had left his old shell inside the bathhouse. She felt that the ritual had brought them closer together, had made them accomplices. They drank tea with honey, tea from the petals of flowers, on that night of transformations, that night of revelations. They were not able to speak. The weight of the full moon made their silence more immense; and now, immersed anew in the outside world, in battle plans and the world of intrigues, they connected in some other manner, communicated their thoughts differently.

❧

Migration is an act of survival. Malinalli wished she could have relied on the lightness of butterflies and migrated on time, flown through the high skies, far above the clouds, where she would not have to hear weeping and lamenting, where you could not distinguish the mutilated corpses, the rivers of blood, the smell of death. She wanted to flee before her eyes grew blind, before her heart froze and her spirit disconnected from her gods.

Cortés had decided to move on and slaughter the inhabitants of Cholula, which he considered an act of self-defense. He wanted to prevent any act before he could be caught defenseless. He wanted to teach a lesson to the natives who were harboring thoughts against him and, at the same time, send a clear message to Montezuma.

He brought together the lords of Cholula in the temple of Quetzalcóatl, under the pretext of saying his good-byes and thanking them for their services. Malinalli and Aguilar served as translators for the three thousand men who came there. Once they were inside, the doors were closed. Cortés, on his horse, spoke powerfully, his voice like thunder, like the earth when it quakes. His figure, magnified by the height of his horse, was imposing.

During the Middle Ages, only noblemen rode horses, and for that reason, Cortés, a plebeian, liked to give orders on his horse. It made him into a superior being, physically and socially speaking. Cortés chastised the Cholultecans for wanting to murder him, when he had arrived in Cholula as a peacemaker and the only thing he had done since that day was to warn them against the error of worshipping false idols, of committing acts of sodomy, and of performing human sacrifices. Malinalli, when translating, tried to be true to his words, and so that everyone heard her, she raised her voice as much as possible. She spoke in the name of Malinche, a nickname they had given Cortés, since he always had her by his side. Malinche in some way meant the master of Malinalli.

"Malinche is very upset. He wants to know if perhaps you want to sneak behind our backs, do as the slithery, the stormy, and the deceitful. If you want to lay on us your shields, your clubs, when all Malinche did was come in peace? When all his words attempted to do was to speak to you of that which would expand your hearts? He, who brings the word of our Lord, never expected you to be plotting his murder. He, who sees and knows all, cannot ignore that in the outskirts of Cholula there are Mexica warriors ready to attack."

The chiefs confessed to all, but justified their actions by saying they were only obeying orders from Montezuma. Cortés then mentioned the laws of the Spanish realm, where treason was punishable by death, and therefore the lords of Cholula deserved death. Malinalli had not yet finished translating these last words when the discharge of a harquebus signaled the beginning of the slaughter. For over two hours the Spaniards stabbed, beat, and murdered all the Indians who were gathered there. Malinalli ran to a corner to hide and with eyes filled with horror watched Cortés and his soldiers sever arms, ears, and heads. The sound of the metal ripping through muscle and bone, the screams, the wailing, terrorized her heart. The beautiful *huipil* that she was wearing was soon splattered with blood. Blood soaked the feathered crests, the clothes, and the mantles of the Cholultecans. It gathered in pools. Mortar and shotgun fire tore to pieces the terrorized multitude. No one could escape, no one could scale the walls. Defenseless, they were all murdered.

When all the men gathered there had been killed, the doors to the courtyard were opened and Malinalli fled in terror. The five thousand Tlaxcaltecans and the more than four hundred Cempoalans allied with Cortés pillaged and plundered the city. Malinalli dodged them and ran until she reached the river, horrified by the hatred with which they slaughtered men, women, and children. The temple of Huitzilopochtli, the god who represented Mexica dominion, was set on fire. The frenzy of murder, plunder, and blood lasted for two days, until Cortés reestablished order. A total of six thousand Cholultecans perished. Cortés ordered the few priests who survived to wash the floors and walls, to rid the temples of idols and in their place to install crosses and images of the Virgin Mary.

According to Cortés, this horror was a good thing, so that all of the Indians could see and realize that their idols were false and deceitful, that they could not protect them adequately because instead of being gods, they were demons. For Cortés, the conquest was a struggle of good against evil, of the true god against false gods, of superior beings against inferior beings. He thought that he had the sacred mission of saving all the Indians from the ignorance in which they lived, which, according to him led them to commit all types of savage and uncivilized acts.

The thousands of dismembered corpses, lifeless, purposeless, weighed heavily on Malinalli's spirit. Her soul was no longer her own; it had been captured during the struggle by all those silent, defenseless, unspared bodies. No one, neither the troops of Spaniards, nor the troops of natives, caused her any harm; no one damaged her body; no one wounded her; she was, however, dead and she bore on her shoulders the weight of hundreds of the dead. Her eyes had no life in them, they no longer shone, her breath could scarcely be felt, her heartbeat was weak. She went a long while without moving a single muscle. She was freezing to death, but she wasn't the least bit motivated to cover herself with a blanket. Besides, she was sure that she would not be able to find a single one that was not covered with blood. The October cold penetrated her bones, her soul. She, who had always lived on the coast, blessed by the heat of the sun, was suffering from the change of temperature, but much more so by what her eyes had witnessed.

Suddenly, the sound of footsteps jolted her. Her heart expected the worst. She turned around to see who it was that approached her, and found Cortés's horse. Alone, without its master, approaching the river to drink. The horse also seemed frightened. Its legs were stained with blood. Malinalli went to him and tried to clean them. The horse remained still, letting her do her work. When she was finished, Malinalli caressed its head, looked into its large eyes and saw her own fear reflected there. The same thing seemed to be happening to the horse. He looked at Malinalli in an odd manner. Neither of them seemed to recognize each other, for they were no longer the same; events had changed them. Malinalli was no longer the girl-woman delighted to be baptized whom the horse had seen some months back.

That horse who had been present at her rebirth during the baptism had now been a witness to death. This was some other Malinalli, some other river, some other Cholula, some other Cortés. Malinalli remembered Cortés's hands and she shuddered. She had seen the cruelty of those hands. She had seen how those hands that on the day before had caressed her, were capable of killing with such resolve. She could never see him in the same way again. Nothing was the same and there was no going back. What would come in response to this massacre that she herself felt responsible for? She tried to justify herself, thinking that although she had not confided in Cortés about her conversation with the Cholultecan woman—who had offered to flee with her son and Malinalli before the Spaniards were wiped out—Cortés had found out about the plans by other means. Moreover, Cortés's allies had informed him, before she said anything, that hidden traps had been set up on the streets and pathways, with pointed stakes at the bottom to impale the horses, that some streets were bricked off, that they were stockpiling stones on the rooftop terraces, and that the women and children were being evacuated. The Tlaxcaltecans had also informed him that on the outskirts of the city, there was a garrison of fifteen to twenty thousand of Montezuma's warriors gathered, something that was never confirmed. Only one fact remained: the Spaniards along with the Tlaxcaltecans had slaughtered more than six thousand natives. And she could be next.

She no longer felt safe with anyone. If at one point in the beginning she felt joy at having been chosen as "The Tongue" and offered the promise of freedom in exchange for her labors as translator, now there was no guarantee of her longed-for liberty. What kind of freedom were they referring to? What could guarantee that those who respected nothing would respect her life? What could a man who killed with such cruelty offer her? What kind of god would allow so many innocents to be slaughtered in his name? She understood nothing, could find no purpose or meaning.

They had taught her to serve. In her position as a slave, she had done nothing but serve her masters. And she could do it efficiently. In translating and interpreting, she had only followed the orders of her Spanish masters, to whom she had been given and whom she had to serve promptly. For a time, she had been convinced that her good merits as a slave, as a servant, would not only help her achieve her yearned-for freedom but also accomplish a positive change for everyone else. She, in fact, had believed that the Spanish god was the true god and that he was nothing else but a new manifestation of Quetzalcóatl, who had come to make clear that he did not need men to die on the sacrificial stone. But the way she had seen the Spanish act left her desolate, destitute, disillusioned and, above all, horrified. The obvious question was, who was she going to serve? And more important, why? What was the point of living in a world that was losing its meaning? What kind of person continued?

She didn't even have the comfort of seeking refuge in her gods, because, to be fair, she had to admit that Quetzalcóatl had done nothing to defend his followers. The truth was that she, as well as the Cholultecans, had thought up to the last minute that Quetzalcóatl would reveal himself, that he would flood Cholula, that he would find some way to defend his faithful. But he was never heard from. A feeling of vulnerability seized Malinalli. Suddenly, all her fears and all her guilt took up arms in her heart. They struggled to be acknowledged, valued, and accepted. The eternal fear of abandonment, of loss, of being an unwanted girl, not appreciated or taken into account, presented itself more forcefully than ever before. It had been reborn! It had a new name, a new identity, new gods, but she did not yet know how it was going to punish her.

Yes, she felt that she deserved a punishment, she had always felt it. She had never understood why, but each time that she had been given away, she had felt in the depth of her heart that it was because of a wrong that she had committed, perhaps the simple act of being a woman, or some other thing, but that was how she felt and that was how she experienced it, as an immense punishment. Now she understood less what was happening, her mind unable to absorb so many changes in so little time.

So many words, so many ideas. The one that proved the most difficult to understand was the devil as the incarnation of evil. The concept that the devil was a fallen angel, distant from the mercy of the heavenly father and condemned to live in darkness—who at the same time had the power to do away with all of divine creation—was never very clear to her. If he had such power, why didn't he use it? And if to do it he needed for men to open their hearts to him, then he wasn't as powerful as they said. What kind of a demon was he? On the other hand, was the true god so dimwitted that he had created a power capable of destroying him? And was he so weak that each moment he risked that his children would forget him and give in to sin? No, she could not at all understand the Spaniards' ideas about good and evil.

For her, the spiritual world had an intimate relationship with Nature and the cosmos, with their rhythm, with the movement of the stars through the skies. When the Sun and the Moon had been born in Teotihuacan, they had freed mankind from the darkness. She knew from her ancestors that the light emitted by the stars was not only physical, but spiritual as well, and that their passage through the heavens served to unify the thoughts of men, the cycles of time and space. The contemplation of the skies, like a game of mirrors, became an internal contemplation, an instrument of transformation. It was something that happened inside and out, in the sky and in the earth. Year after year, cycle after cycle, interlacing it, as if dealing with a bed of snakes, in this manner incorporating oneself into the fabric of life, where it is not necessary to die to go to heaven, but only to be intimately bound with the earth in order to remain in the presence of the gods, for whosoever dedicated themselves to observing the ordered proceedings of the sky, was made into a sun, into a god.

She did not understand a god that you could not see in the sky—like the Sun—with your own eyes, a god with which you could not become one, a god outside of time, in another heaven where only those free from sin could enter. A vengeful god, a destructive god whom she feared and did not want to annoy, but could not fathom how to avoid doing so. She didn't know what to do from now on. She felt like dust scattered in the wind, like a feather without the *quetzal*, like a husk without grains of corn, with no purpose, no desire, no life. Why had she been born? To help the Spaniards destroy her world, her cities, her beliefs, and her gods? She refused to accept it. There had to be another reason. She had to find a new meaning for her life. To see the world in a different manner. She had to stop seeing the past in each river, each stone, each plant, each *huipil*, in each tortilla that she brought to her mouth. She had to see things in the way the Spaniards did. Her life depended on it, because it was clear that up to that moment they had never been speaking about the same thing, had never seen the same thing nor wanted the same thing. The change that she wished for her people was simply to put an end to human sacrifice, but she expected everything else to remain the same, especially when it came to the cult of Quetzalcóatl. Of course, she understood that it wasn't about what she wanted or had wanted. Nobody cared about her opinion and for the moment she didn't care to return to the city to see what was left of the great Cholula.

Standing beside the horse, she was silent for a long while. Neither of them had plans to do anything. Some butterflies approached them. They were spattered with blood. Malinalli wept without tears, for there were no more left in her eyes. She wanted to escape so as not to see, not to hear, not to know. Her mind took flight and found itself outside of time with her grandmother, on the day that she had taken her to a sanctuary of monarch butterflies.

⊰◦❀◦⊱

It had been a joyful spring day. Malinalli was dressed all in white with necklaces of feathers and jade bracelets and anklets. She was excited, for her grandmother had told her that the butterflies had returned and she was taking her to see them. The child did not understand why they left each year or why they returned and, curious, she asked her grandmother why the butterflies didn't stay in their homes so that she could see them all year long. The grandmother explained that the butterflies, like so many winged creatures, were great travelers and that this was good, for moving with the wind is what makes one change, renew, become stronger. Each journey of the butterfly was a struggle for life. They migrated in search of food and a climate that would allow them to survive the cold winters; otherwise they would perish. This way they fulfilled a promise of life.

Her grandmother explained to her that within the human body we all had a traveling butterfly buried in our pelvic bone. That was the bone that symbolized them.

"When the flower opens, the butterfly comes," her grandmother said. "When the butterfly comes, the flower opens."

This meant that the energy generated by the butterfly, at a certain moment, liberated itself from its source and flew upward through the innards of the bone through the spinal column until it reached the bones of the skull, which symbolized the celestial dome. This journey was a repetition of the one that Quetzalcóatl had taken on the moment of his initiation and his transformation into the Morning Star. Whoever went through it, like him, became a god. And for the grandmother the return of the butterflies to their sanctuary anticipated the eventual return of Quetzalcóatl.

The child was very excited about the trip, overcome at the prospect of seeing so many butterflies. Malinalli's mother had been opposed to the idea of the journey, saying that it would be impossible for the blind old woman to endure such a trip, and on top of that, to care for Malinalli, who according to her was such a restless and disobedient child. The trip would have been canceled had the grandmother not argued energetically and forcefully that to travel to sacred places it was not necessary to see, and that her years did not matter, for fatigue did not exist there, and that no one was going to stop her or convince her not to go, because aside from everything else, it was important for Malinalli to come to know the origin and eternal return of life's creation.

"And I will not die in peace, nor leave this world, until I have made this journey with my granddaughter."

So she asserted, and thus, hand in hand, Malinalli and her grandmother left on the road to the sanctuary on the first day of spring. They walked for three days, resting in small towns along the way, where they joined a group of men and women who were traveling to the sanctuary, to the ritual of initiation where, each spring, the wind and the abundance of elements are summoned so that people may obtain from the earth and the skies the riches necessary to fulfill their tasks.

During their pilgrimage they passed through a town where men and women dedicated themselves to the carving of stone, projecting on them the image of all the gods, all the suns, and the graven thoughts that would become eternally scripted into the stone. This task fascinated Malinalli, who learned that even the hardest thing was malleable and that the entire universe was flexible to goodwill. The child then asked the grandmother if, since there was a butterfly inside the body, there were also stones like these.

"Like these? Mmmnn . . . Not like these, no. But sometimes the heart of a person can turn to stone. On the one hand it is good to be firm, not to be shaken up by any little thing, but it is not good to be too hard, for it will take longer to understand the truth, to be set afire with love."

That night they slept in the town. Malinalli gathered stones of all sizes and saved them to take with her.

One day they came upon the fossil of a seashell.

"What is this?" the girl asked, placing the seashell in the

grandmother's hand, who, feeling it, immediately answered as if she were seeing it:

"It is a memory in stone."

"Did they make it here?"

"No," the grandmother responded with a laugh, "it was made by Mother Earth, it is her work."

Malinalli saved it also in her sack and they kept walking. Bearing so much weight, the girl soon grew tired and pretended that she could not go on for her knees and her feet were in great pain. Her grandmother paid no attention to her, didn't stop, didn't sympathize, kept on going. Malinalli felt as if her grandmother could disappear forever and ran as never before in order to catch up with her.

"I am very excited to see the butterflies," she said, after she had reached her grandmother. "But why do we have to walk so much?"

"Your task is to walk," the grandmother replied. "A still body limits itself to itself, a body in movement expands, becomes a part of everything. But you have to learn to walk lightly, not with heavy steps. Walking fills us with energy and changes us to allow us to look into the secret of things. Walking transforms us into butterflies that rise and see truly what the world is. What life is. What our body is. It is the eternity of consciousness. It is the understanding of all things. That is god within us. But if you want, you can remain sitting, and turn into stone."

As a response to this, the girl took out of her sack all the stones that she had gathered and grabbed her grandmother's hand to keep walking.

Malinalli did not complain again. A short time before arriving, they rested from the midday sun inside a cave with an echo. The girl was amazed when she found the echo returning her words. The grandmother explained that this was why it was so important to honor the word. Each sound that we emit travels through the air, but it always returns to us. If we want the right words to resound in our ears, all we have to do is pronounce them beforehand.

On the fourth day, they reached the sanctuary of the monarch butterflies. There was a great crowd. Everyone had arrived from different regions, spoke different dialects, had different customs and habits, but one thing brought them together—the sacred ritual of witnessing the flight of the butterflies who, with the mingling of their forms in flight, sketched sacred codices in the air, messages from the gods and songs that only the soul could hear. It was amazing to see thousands of butterflies gathered around a giant tree, flying all over the place, emitting light from the air.

"Why are all the butterflies together?" Malinalli asked, brimming with enthusiasm.

"They come together to unite distances, to unite the cold with the heat," the grandmother explained. "They are together so that we may read what they project with their forms. Study their shapes, their movements, their sounds, concentrate on them."

The little four-year-old girl went into a sort of trance. She stopped seeing the butterflies and instead saw codices, manifestations of sacred art, as if she was one sent by the gods, a child prophet. Her mind understood how to read the codices without anyone having to explain, without them having to be there. She saw all of them and understood their meaning.

"What do you see?" the grandmother asked.

"Codices," the girl responded.

"And if you close your eyes, do you still see them?"

"Yes."

"Well then, now open your eyes. Do you still see them?"

"No," Malinalli asserted.

"This shows that you are awake, and don't live in illusions. You will see what you wish to see."

❖

Now she wanted to forget. She didn't want the images of the destruction of Cholula to sketch a codex in her mind. She wanted to forget the day in the bathhouse also, in which she believed that Quetzalcóatl had moistened Cortés with the memory of god. She no longer wanted to speak, to see, to struggle for her freedom. Not at such a price. Not through the death of so many innocents, so many children, so many women. She rather wished that serpents would come out of her womb and wrap themselves around her body, that they would suffocate her, leave her without breath, turn her into nothing, a word in the moistness of the tongue, a symbol, a hieroglyph, a stone.

SIX

The cold was unbearable. They had been walking for days. Cortés stubbornly insisted on reaching Tenochtitlán at whatever the cost. After having lost their way various times, he found out that they had been given false information on how to reach the great city of the Mexicas, and so, against all advice, he decided to cross between Popocatépetl and Iztaccíhuatl, the volcanoes that watched over the valley of Anáhuac.

The path was almost four thousand meters above sea level. It was November, and the cold was hellish, if such an adjective may be used. According to what they had told Malinalli, in hell there was an eternal fire that caused eternal suffering, and this image appealed to her, to equate such cold with hell. She could not imagine a time when it would go away. She felt it under her skin, in her bones. Her teeth chattered like bells during a feast day. Some of the Cuban servants that had come with the Spanish had already died due to the weather.

Malinalli was convinced that her hour would soon come. She was very tired. Her feet felt as if they did not belong to her, she could not feel them. They were completely frozen, numb. So much so, that she could not feel the wounds from the giant open blisters on her toes, caused by wearing closed shoes which she had taken from one of the Cuban slaves who had died along the way. She did not mind using a dead person's shoes. She would do anything to relieve the cold in her feet. The problem was that she had never worn closed shoes, and before long she was already blistered and in great pain, but was not allowed to stop. She kept on going despite the bleeding blisters, until she could no longer feel pain in her stiffened feet.

Now she was only drowsy, very drowsy. She was incapable of conceiving of a sunny, warm, and joyful day. She wanted to imagine the heat that she felt all over her body during the summer days, but it was impossible. She so much needed to warm her skin! Not knowing why, she thought of grasshoppers.

Every summer, she used to catch them in the cornfields. She liked surprising them in mid-hop. She kept them in a small gourd, and later, in the communal kitchen, would drop them into boiling water. It was an instantaneous death for the grasshoppers. Afterward, she rinsed them till the water was completely clear and roasted them in a ceramic pot. There was nothing more delicious than a handful of roasted grasshoppers on a summer afternoon, after having bathed and played in the river's cold waters.

At that moment, she wished with all her soul to be a grasshopper, so someone would catch her and throw her into a pot of boiling water. To be heat, to be fire, instead of a wounded aching body. If she had to die for this, then let it be. She didn't care. At least she would die nice and warm, her spirit would be absorbed by the sun, and her body, which would remain on the earth, would become succulent food. Her flesh would delight others. She thought that the best thing, considering the taste buds of the Spaniards, would be for them to season her with a bit of crushed garlic, that plant that they had brought with them, that they ate so often that she could smell it in their sweat and on their breath. The cravings were killing her! At that moment she would have given anything for a roasted grasshopper. But in this cold, it would be impossible to find one. And now she knew why. In this weather the only thing one wanted was to cover oneself under the earth and not go hopping here and there. Malinalli could not walk any further. She remembered the journey that she had taken with her grandmother, and the words that she had been told on that occasion resonated in her mind.

"You task is to walk. Walking transforms us into butterflies that rise and see truly what the world is."

Through her own experience, Malinalli knew that ritual walking effectively caused a detachment from the body, a spiritual elevation, an assimilation with everything. It is what happened when you defeated the body, when you triumphed over it, when the flesh renounced the walker and allowed her to integrate herself into the nothing where everything is, where all is found. Malinalli, completely exhausted, closed her eyes to see if she could become one with her grandmother, but she wasn't able to. Her body kept her prisoner.

Cortés watched her from a distance. They had decided to rest and wait for Diego de Ordaz's expedition to return from Popocatépetl. Cortés had sent ten scouts under Diego de Ordaz's command to explore Popocatépetl up close. The volcano, according to what he had been told, had erupted several times in the past few years. For most of the conquistadors, the sight of an active volcano was something new that they did not want to miss.

After he had rested, Cortés watched the cloud of smoke and ash that rose from the volcano. Then his glance turned to Malinalli. Cortés watched her closely. With her eyes closed, huddled under a blanket lent to her by Bernal Díaz del Castillo, she seemed small, vulnerable, but still not far away from the truth. Hernán pondered on how admirable a woman she was. She had not complained once. She kept pace with all of them without uttering a word. She had never fallen ill, or wept, or become an annoyance. It was impossible not to compare her to his wife. Catalina Xuárez was a weak and sickly woman, who had not been able to give him children. He was sure that his wife, Catalina, if placed in the same position as Malinalli, would already be dead.

Cortés was in turn being watched by Malinalli, out of the corner of her eye. She didn't want to speak with anyone, so she pretended to be asleep. She didn't even have any energy to ask for help. She liked watching Cortés's body, his build, his strength, his courage, his audacity, his gift as a leader. Thousands of times, standing on the shore and meditating on the eternal return of the tides, she had wished for the return of her father, or someone like him, who could protect her. At that moment, she asked herself if Cortés could be that man and she decided that he couldn't be. The protection that she longed for had nothing to with her annihilation as a person. The protection and defense that the Spaniards said they would provide against false gods and pagan practices had more or less left them in a defenseless state, made them into weak children who did not know what was good for them and who needed someone superior to tell them. To be protected by Cortés would undeniably mark her as a weak and ignorant woman.

But she was so tired that she did not want to think about anything except the sun. It was not in vain that her ancestors had said that first came the fire and from it, was made the sun, and from it mankind. The sun was fire in motion. She closed her eyes. The altitude was ravaging her well-being. She had a headache and felt that there was not enough air to breathe. She was as dizzy as when her grandmother lifted her by the arms and spun her around and around like the flying men of Papantla, those men who created beautiful dances in the air as they fell to the ground held up by ropes tied around their ankles. There were five members altogether, of which four descended toward the ground, little by little, twisting and turning as they fell, while the fifth remained up above the great pole, signifying the center. The four dancers that flew through the air represented each of the cardinal points. Malinalli saw them various times in her youth, and she loved when her grandmother made her into a flying dancer, grabbing her by the feet and making her spin. When her grandmother tired, she would spin and spin with open arms on her own till she grew dizzy and fell to the ground laughing.

The grandmother explained to her that this happened because she had lost her center.

"God is in the center, there where there is no shape at all, no sound, no movement. Whenever you are dizzy, sit down, stop moving, remain silent, and you will find Our Lord there, in your invisible center, that which unites you with him. We are like the beads in the necklace of creation, and we are joined one to the other, each taking up the place and space that corresponds to us. When you stumble to one side or the other, you alter the order of the skies and the sky opens, the earth opens. When you get separated like that you will not fall where you are meant to fall, you will not walk where you are meant to walk, you will not die where you were meant to die, because the cord has been broken, because everything is part of everything else and everything affects everything else. Because of this, god grows sorrowful when we do not see him, when we do not recognize him, when we go through our lives with our backs to him."

"Where is god? How can I see him?"

"To see the invisible is complicated, but you should know that he for whom we live is in the air we breathe, in each drop of water, each body, each plant, each animal, in all forms of his creation. In the center, in the invisible in all things, is where you can find him. Each celestial body is united in its center with the other stars and with us. It's as if a silver string had linked us together at the time of creation. To see the invisible in others is to see god in them. To listen to the invisible in their words is to listen to god. To feel the water in the air before it rains is to feel god. It doesn't matter how different the faces that you see are, how different each one's song is; beyond the body, beyond their words, dwells the lord of all things. That is why performance, song, movement, and everything we do is so important. If we do it according to our center, according to divinity, it will have a sacred quality; if we do it dizzily, it will throw us to the ground, cast us aside, disconnected from god. We all spin. Each man, each moon, each sun, each star spins around its center. The movement of stars is sacred and so is ours. It unites us to the same invisible."

But perhaps the most important thing that her grandmother's knowledge passed on to Malinalli was the notion that behind each divine representation—whether it be in paper, in stone, in flower, or in song—god dwelled. The shape, the color, and the sound that was chosen to represent them did not matter.

"My sweet Malinalli, even before you took the shape of this body you were already one with god and you will remain so even when your form is erased from the earth."

Later, she continued.

"When I die, when I will be outside of time, it will be difficult to see me, to hear me, to feel me, and that is why I am going to give you this Tonantzin stone. She is our mother, and you can ask her whatever you desire. I will be dancing in the sky near her and we will both be watching you."

And now Malinalli took in her fingers the ceramic bead necklace with the image of Tonantzin that she had made with her grandmother, and asked that her center be restored, to control the dizziness that was driving her mad and to help her regain her well-being. There wasn't a long way to go before they reached the Valley of Anáhuac. She wanted to see it. She wanted to survive. After making this wish, her eyes closed. Malinalli left her body and was converted into thought, idea, dream. She had no problem interweaving her thoughts with the other slaves, and she instantly experienced an unimaginable freedom. She knew that she had settled into another reality, and that what she saw was part of a dream, but she also knew that in that dream she could discover a better reality, a reality more collective than individual.

In her dream she saw herself as part of a united feminine mind that was having the same dream. In the dream, a group of barefoot women walked over the ice of a river that had frozen at the moment the light of the moon had been reflected on its surface. The soles of their feet cracked open when coming in contact with the ice, and the wounds formed stellar maps. The light of the full moon fell forcefully on all of them and they became one mind, one body, they were all one woman holding herself up in the wind and nourished on the faith of all who want to free themselves from the nightmare of sensation, of touching, of weeping, of loving, of bleeding, of dying, of having, and of letting go. Malinalli, in the body of this unified woman, saw herself surrounded by a dozen moons and held up by the antlers of a thirteenth one. With her hands she picked up prayers and pieces of pain that she made into roses. Later she felt the moon underneath her feet completely afire and the flames devoured her thoughts. Her mind was a blaze that created images that nailed themselves into the hearts of men like blades of fire, as they spoke to them of the true meaning of language. When Malinalli felt that the moon, now beside her, was completely ablaze, she opened her eyes. There were tears there, and in her heart a premonition of flowers.

❄❂❄

Malinalli was this, reflection of a reflection. The light of the moon fell at her back, and the lengthening shadow that left her body covered a great part of the distance that separated her from the Stone of the Sun, located in the Great Temple of Tenochtitlán.

Malinalli had decided to go out in the middle of the night to stroll in the Plaza in silence, without having to translate or interpret, without having to feign indifference before the gods of her ancestors, so that she would not be marked an idolator. They had arrived in Tenochtitlán the day before and Malinalli had been as impressed as the Spaniards, if not more so, with the great city's beauty. The Great Temple was the center. It was the place that reflected the vision of the universe of its founders. From that place originated great avenues toward the four cardinal points.

There, standing before the Stone of the Sun, Malinalli was at the exact center of the city, the universe. The Sun, the Moon, she herself, and the Stone of the Sun created all that was unique and indivisible and at that moment she understood that the Stone was an image of the invisible, that it was a circle that represented not only the Sun and the Winds, the forces of creation, but the invisible at its center.

For the first time she saw the invisible and she understood that time was something different than what she had thought. She was used to understanding the passing of time through the movement of the stars in the skies, through the cycles of sowing and reaping, of life and death. When she sewed she could also understand time. A beautiful *huipil* was proof of time inverted, of the way that time is interwoven. In each embroidery, Malinalli gave her time to others and shared with them beauty.

It had been a long time since she had had time to sew, much less embroider. Her life alongside the Spaniards had changed her concept of time completely. Now she measured it by the days of the march, by the number of words translated, by the number of intrigues and strategies developed. Her experience of time seemed to have been accelerated, and it did not leave her a single free moment to place herself at the center of knowledge. It was a confusing time, in which her time and Cortés's time were ineluctably interconnected, laced, tied together. It was as if through a native custom, in a traditional ceremony, someone had tied the ends of their vestments together and made them man and wife. It was an uneasy feeling. Feeling tied down stole her freedom. She wanted to go one way and Cortés veered toward the other. It was an enforced union that she had not decided on but that seemed to mark her always. Her time was without fail now interwoven with Cortés's time. But that night, before the Stone of the Sun, Malinalli felt balanced, restored, at one with time, or even better, outside of it.

That night, Montezuma also reflected on the concept of time, his time, and the cycle that was ending. Like Malinalli, he could not sleep. He went out to the palace balcony and from there watched a resplendent woman, dressed in white, who was crossing the plaza. His heart jumped. She looked like Cihuacóatl, the sixth disastrous omen, who appeared at nights and wandered through the streets of the great city, weeping and letting out great yelps for her children. Moreover, he very clearly heard a voice that said, My little ones, we must flee! Where will I take you, so sorrow cannot reach us? He felt goose bumps. The sight left him frozen. He wanted to move, but could not. He tried to calm down, to rein in his thoughts, but they did nothing but lead him to images of misfortune. Not exactly sure why, he thought of the strange bird with a mirror in its head that years before some fishermen had brought to the palace. The finding of the bird was the last of the ill omens. As soon as Montezuma looked at the bird, it disappeared from his sight. He tried to remember what was reflected, and in place of the memory, a tremendously painful image came to his mind: of a heavy rain falling on the Stone of the Sun. And each drop of rain that fell on the stone wore it down, leaving it completely smooth. Montezuma then understood that death was everything that had no meaning and could not be measured, and he shuddered. His time had definitely ended and he feared for the future of his children, especially the younger ones, Tecuichpo, who was nine, and Axayácatl, who was seven.

❦

Extending this strange game of mirrors, Malinalli's fear for her children reflected that of Montezuma, with the difference that she had yet to have them. It was a night of magic, of light, of peace, before the war. Malinalli returned to this world on hearing the splashing of fish that were jumping in the canals surrounding the Great Plaza. With each jump, they made a sound similar to a stone falling into the water, but the noise of the fish was more delicate, continuous, and calming. Fish jumped on a night of the full moon because of the light. Thanks to the brilliance of the moon reflected in the water, the fish could see the insects flittering on its surface and jumped up to devour them. Malinalli expected that in the same manner, Tlazolteotl, the "devourer of filth," would eat up her sins, or what she thought of as sins, which were nothing more than nonconformity, misfortune, a series of contrary feelings.

Immediately she went into the temple of Huitzilopochtli, God of War, a place where she knew she could find the goddess, for Tlazolteotl didn't have a temple of her own. She was a lunar deity, the goddess of passionate love, of those who unleashed lust and broke the laws against adultery. She was also the great pregnant mother, the patron saint of births, of medicines, and steam baths that cleanse and purify more than the body. This goddess was feared, for just as easily as she set on passion and sexual appetite, she could take them away or cause venereal diseases. To prevent all of this, if you committed a sexual transgression, it was necessary to confess to one of the goddess's priests, who in her name received "the filth" and mandated a penance that could be anything from a simple four-day fast to the perforation of the tongue with an agave thorn. Since the fast had to take place during the four days preceding the celebration of the Chihuateteos, the feminine deities that had died during childbirth, and this date had already passed, Malinalli decided on her own that the punishment that befitted her case was perforation of the tongue.

Of course, she didn't confess to any priest. She couldn't, for Cortés had not approved it, and she immediately realized that he would not approve of having her tongue perforated. What excuse could she give the day after, when she couldn't talk? There had to be another way for her to punish herself, but she couldn't find it. She felt dirty, sinful. She longed to cleanse her soul. So that she wouldn't be seen, she had gone looking for relief at that hour of night. Recent events had left her feeling pained, overwhelmed, and anxious.

First of all, there was the fact that during the first meeting between Montezuma and Cortés she had been the translator and during her performance she had looked directly into the eyes of Montezuma, the great governor. The Supreme Ruler. Her legs had shaken. Looking at his face had been an act of great transgression. She knew perfectly well that it was prohibited to look at Montezuma's countenance and that whoever did so was condemned to death. And yet, she did it. The look that she got in return indicated that Montezuma did not like her attitude at all, but instead of showing his annoyance, he allowed her to continue to translate his welcome speech. Malinalli did it reverently. She considered it the greatest honor of her life to transmit Montezuma's words. What she never expected was that Montezuma would dispossess his throne in favor of Cortés, and that she, being the translator, would be the one who practically handed Cortés his kingdom. She also did not imagine the profound sorrow she would feel on doing so. It was sad to realize that her faith meant nothing when compared to Montezuma's. To see an emperor, a man who had been educated for power, give up his kingdom, moved her deeply. To be a witness to Montezuma's intense faith, to the spiritual grandeur that allowed him to detach himself from his tremendous power before a spirit: that of Quetzalcóatl. To feel Montezuma's pride at being the emperor who was chosen to witness Quetzalcóatl's return caused her to shudder. Only a man who had been spiritually transformed could undertake such an exchange.

To see Montezuma offer his kingdom, not to a person,

nor a face, nor an ambition, but to the spirit of Quetzalcóatl, was in and of itself, a mystical, sacred act. And Malinalli knew in her heart that Quetzalcóatl was truly grateful, truly welcomed, wherever he was, even though it was not in Cortés's body. As she translated Montezuma's speech, Malinalli also experienced a spiritual transformation and acted as a true mediator between this and the other world. Her voice rose forcefully from her chest.

"O Our Lord," she told Cortés, "thou art welcomed. Thou hast reached thy land, thy city, thy home Mexico. Thou hast come to sit on thy throne . . . which I, in thy name, have possessed for some time. Other lords, now dead, possessed it before me: the lords Itzcóatl, Montezuma the Elder, Axayácatl, Tizoc, and Ahuizotl. Oh, how brief was the time that they kept and dominated the city of Mexico for you. Under their wings, under the mantle of their power, the people lived. . . . Oh, how I wish one of them would come and see; he would be amazed at what I now see before me. Me, the remaining one, the survivor of all our lords.

"Our Lord, I am neither sleeping, nor dreaming. With my eyes I see thy face and thy person. For days have I been expecting this, for days has my heart been looking at those parts whence thou came.

"Thou emerged from among the clouds and the mists of the place hidden to everyone. This is certainly what the kings who came before us had said, that thou wouldst prepare to return and reign in these kingdoms, that thou wouldst sit on thy throne. Now I see that what has been said is come to pass.

"Be thou welcome. Thou must needs have endured great labors coming from so far. Rest now! Here is thy house, and thy palaces; take them and rest in them with all thy captains and companions that thou hast brought with thee."

A great silence fell from the sky in response. Cortés could not believe what he was hearing. Without firing a single bullet, he had been invited to be ruler of those immense and rich lands.

The more than four thousand nobles and principal lords of the Mexica kingdom, dressed in their finest outfits, their best skins, feathers, and precious gems, were also amazed at these words.

Cortés asked Malinalli to translate these words in response: "Tell Montezuma to take comfort, not to be afraid. That I love him very much, as do all who come with me. No one will do him any harm. We have been filled with great joy on seeing you and meeting you, something we have looked forward to for many days. Our wish has been fulfilled."

Montezuma then took Cortés's arm and in procession, followed by his brother Cuitláhuac and the lords Cacama of Tezcoco; Tetlepanquetzal, the prince of Tlacopan, Itzcuauhtzin of Tlatelolco, and others, headed for Tenochtitlán.

Tenochtitlán was a city whose expanse was double that of any city in Spain. On seeing it, Cortés did not know what to say. He had never seen a city like it, constructed in the middle of a lake and surrounded by wide canals through which hundreds of canoes glided.

Cortés was dazzled by the mirrors of water. He was impressed by the simple and majestic vision of an architecture that seemed to have been designed in the stars, an architecture that at the same time moved him and awoke in him anger over not having had the talent to imagine it. The contemplation of the great buildings moved all of them, beckoned them to give themselves to the city, to embrace it. But at the same time, the envy that rose in them made them want to reject the city, vaporize it, volatilize it, erase it. In them, a struggle between reverence and scorn was set loose. The more they made themselves at home in Tenochtitlán, the more their admiration and anger grew. The Mexica architecture, aside from making obvious the degree of development of this great civilization, stirred in them devotion, astonishment, respect, for its buildings possessed great harmony and magnificence.

Cortés and his people were housed in the Palace of Axayácatl, the former governor, and father to Montezuma. It was a one-story rectangular building, with many inner courtyards and gardens. Some of them housed wild beasts and exotic plants, and there were aviaries where Montezuma liked to hunt birds with his blowgun. It was a palatial structure that amazed Cortés, who when settled in his room, sent for Malinalli, with whom he engaged in unbridled fornication as a way of both celebrating his victory and at the same time denying it. As if he had a desire to enjoy himself and attack at the same time, to come closer to the life in Malinalli as a way contemplating his own death. He kissed her mouth, her belly, her thighs, her center, to assuage a longing so feverishly ambitious that he almost broke her in two, wounded her, ripped her apart. When it was over, Malinalli did not want to look into his eyes. She left the palace and washed in one of the canals. Then she waited for night so that she could go without being seen to the temple of Huitzilopochtli. She climbed its one hundred fourteen steps without stopping once to catch her breath. She yearned to confess and do penance. She felt as if she had sinned without meaning to, that what she had felt was not right, that it was not the love that was the reviving energy of life that she had received in her womb.

She knew she did not deserve to be treated thus. Never before had she felt so humiliated. Was that how gods behaved? No. But the worst thing was that she could not tell Montezuma that she had made a mistake, that the Spaniards weren't who he thought they were, that they did not deserve to rule this great city, that they would not know what to do with her. The days that followed confirmed her suspicions. Cortés began to rob—there was no other word for it—as much as he could.

The great works of gold and precious gems were for the most part destroyed as the most beautiful treasures of the decorative arts were taken apart for their gold. The marvelous crests of feathered art were put away and in time many were ruined and eaten by moths.

Before this occurred, there arose a need in Malinalli to save, to protect, to prevent a terrible destruction. She didn't know how she would do it, but she felt as if she and all her civilization were in danger of disappearing. And perhaps because of this she began to value things that before went unnoticed. Her sensibility bloomed and the beauty and majesty of the city kept her in a state of infatuation. She awoke with the hopes of experiencing it and strolling through it, of crossing it by canoe or on foot, of being in it, with it, for it. She continually sought to be alone so that she could wander through the city as she pleased. The market of Tlatelolco was the place that most lured her. The enormous plaza and the crowd of people exchanging products generated a buzzing sound similar to that of a beehive. The humming of the voices resonated as far as a league away. Many of Cortés's soldiers had been in all parts of the world, in Constantinople, in Italy and Rome, and they said that they had never seen "a plaza so large, well stocked, and organized, and so crowded with people."

❧⟨⟩❧

The first time that Malinalli went to the market of Tlatelolco was with Cortés, but since she went in her role as "The Tongue," she was not able to enjoy it. Countless times her feet wanted to stop before many of the fruit stands to buy one, to eat it and savor it, but she couldn't. She had to follow in the steps of her master. So the following day, taking advantage of a meeting her lord had with his captains, she asked for permission to go out, and it was then that she was able to wander through the market as she pleased, to see, touch, and taste everything. She could not enjoy it enough.

She discovered new birds, new fruits, new plants. Everything seduced her, pleased her, stirred her mind. She could not stop imagining what she could create with the feathers and precious metals, the things she could dye with the scarlet cochineals, the things she could sew with those skeins of cotton. In one of the stands, she bartered a cacao seed for a fistful of the longed-for grasshoppers, and she gave free rein to her desires as she strolled through the market of the empire. She gave thanks to the gods for having let her survive the cold of the volcanoes so that she could come to know and enjoy this great city, this memorable market.

Here, all sorts of products from every path and region dominated by the Mexicas were exchanged. The merchants who traveled through the commercial routes with their heavy loads inevitably converged on the market of Tlatelolco. Malinalli at that moment was witness to the great commercial development that had been accomplished during Montezuma's reign.

Then suddenly, Malinalli stopped, her mouth went dry, her stomach turned, and her enjoyment came to a halt. The smell coming from the combination of rabbit fur and quetzal feathers with the smell emitting from plantain leaves, *hoja santa*, turtle eggs, yucca, sweet potato with honey, and vanilla brought to mind the most sorrowful memory of her childhood, the day her mother had given her away to one of the merchants from Xicalango.

Malinalli had been sold as a slave surrounded by aromas very much like these. Her small terrified body did not dare move. Her large moist eyes fixed on a spot where they sold obsidian knives as she listened to what was being offered for her person from some Mayan merchants who had come to the market of Xicalango to sell pots of honey. It hurt to remember that they offered much more for quetzal feathers than they did for her. That part of her past bothered her so much that she decided to erase it in a single stroke. She made up her mind to paint inside her head a new codex, in which she would be the buyer and not an object for sale. In spite of that disagreeable memory, the market continued to be a favorite place to visit. She only had to avoid the spots where they sold slaves, so as not to connect with the memory, and that was that.

Tlatelolco was the heart of the empire. Its veins were the commercial routes through which flowed riches and the most varied products as well as the taxes collected from every province under Mexica control. By all possible means, everything flowed toward the center, towards Tenochtitlán, towards the heart, toward the market of Tlatelolco. That enormous heart registered the pulse of events and was reflected in each and every transaction that took place there. There, Malinalli found out that the prices of cotton blankets and *huipiles* had risen because the Tlaxcaltecans, from the time they had allied themselves with Cortés, had broken old contracts and stopped paying taxes. There Malinalli learned of the indignation of the people, caused not only by the fact that Cortés had been welcomed as a great lord by Montezuma, but that he had been allowed to take over the treasures of the palace of Axayácatl without lifting a finger. Cortés and his men had not only taken the treasures of the past governors, but had even pillaged

Montezuma's private treasures, including the most beautiful feather works and gold—in the shape of crests, breastplates, bangles, nose rings, anklets, bucklers, crowns, wristbands, and ankle bells.

In the courtyards of the palace of Axayácatl, the Spaniards ripped the gold from the feather works and melted them into ingots. At the end of the day, the place looked like a henhouse where precious birds had been plucked. Feathers floated in the air, bereft of their art. They floated everywhere, along with the dreams of those who had imagined them. Some slaves reverently retrieved them and the following day took them to the market to sell them as the feathers that had belonged to the crests of Montezuma, of his father Axayácatl, or of any other king. The people bought them and treasured them, but in doing so their indignation grew and grew, just like the price of obsidian knives and arrows.

There in the market, Malinalli felt the objection of the proud Tenochans, who could not understand or justify to themselves how the emperor Montezuma, their great lord, could not control the sickness for gold that afflicted the foreigners. The talk, the whisperings, and the exclamations of anger all rose dramatically in tone on the day that the Spaniards took Montezuma hostage in reprisal for the death of four of their men at the hands of Quauhpopocatzin, the lord of Nauhtlan, who wanted to prove that the foreigners were not gods, that they died like anyone else, but less honorably. That day, obsidian arrows, cudgels, and shields were raised as the people of Tenochtitlán prepared for war.

The market, as a heart, as a living entity, had a pulse of its own: it slept, awoke, talked, loved, and hated. If it awoke with feelings of war, you could sense it infuriated, vulgar, and violent. If, on the contrary, it awoke in peace, it sounded happy, cheerful, prancing. The change could occur from one day to the next, and from the moment that Cortés overcame Montezuma, the market became a vertiginous play of events. When, in a ceremony, Montezuma swore his obedience to King Charles and accepted his sovereignty over the Mexica people, the market exploded with insults, with cries of rage and pain. When Cortés outlawed human sacrifices and in a violent act climbed to the Temple of Huitzilopochtli, confronted the priests who were guarding it, defeated them, and afterward smashed and shattered the golden mask of the idol with an iron rod, replacing it with an image of the Virgin Mary, the market displayed all the faces of indignation.

The vendors who sold copal pellets were the busiest. Everybody wanted to buy incense to conduct a ceremony of apology in their homes. The market breathed hatred, but after a few days, it regained its tranquility. To calm the mood, Cortés had authorized the feast of Toxcatl, the biggest annual celebration of the Mexica people in honor of their god Huitzilopochtli. The market immediately took in a long breath of air and relaxed. The preparations for the feast began. Amaranth, which was used to make the edible sculptures of the god, filled the air, as did the hummingbird feathers which were used to decorate them. Huitzilopochtli, the sun god of the Mexicas, had been born of a feather placed in the womb of the lady Coatlicue, his mother, and because of this he was represented with the most beautiful feathers.

Malinalli too was excited by the feast. It was the first time that she would experience it. What most attracted her was that Cortés had forbidden human sacrifices during the celebration, so there would not be any spectacle of blood. She had heard that it was an impressive ceremony in which all the nobles and great warriors participated. They performed the dance of the serpent before the Great

Temple as an invocation to the spirit of Coatlicue, mother of Huitzilopochtli. After many hours, the dancers entered a sort of trance, an exaltation of the spirit, through which they put themselves in communion with the generating forces of life, and so the dance took place on two planes, on the earth and in the sky. The serpent danced and flew.

Malinalli felt it a privilege to watch the celebration. She liked being in the great Tenochtitlán, to be a part of it. Sometimes when returning from the market she couldn't help but think how different her fate might have been if instead of giving her away to the merchants of Xicalango, they had pledged her to the services of Montezuma. She would have loved to have been one of his cooks, to have had the privilege to prepare one of the three hundred courses that were cooked in the palace day after day, to seduce him with her culinary skills so that instead of tasting each dish and casting it aside so that his underlings could be fed, he would feel obliged to eat it all, captivated by the mingling of flavors.

It would also have been interesting to have been one of the artisans who created jewels for him, who toyed with metals, who melted gold and silver into anklets, bracelets, earrings, and nose rings. Though as she mulled it over, she thought that the feathered arts would have been, aside from a great honor, her favorite activity, to fashion the capes and crests that the great lord would wear when presiding over ceremonies in the Great Temple. To make feathers—those shadows of the gods—into suns that would outshine the very sun, the lord Huitzilopochtli!

Malinalli then decided to sew feathers on one of her *huipiles* for the occasion. She went to the spot where they sold precious feathers and she noticed a group of people milling around a man. He was one of the many runners who came from the coast bringing fresh seafood for Montezuma. Screaming, he told everyone that ships had arrived with more Spaniards who came in search of Cortés. So Malinalli learned, before Cortés, of the arrival of Pánfilo de Narváez.

Pánfilo arrived at a bad time. The political situation was delicate, complicated. But Cortés had no other choice but to cut him off and detain him, before he himself was arrested and hanged, accused of treason for having disobeyed the orders of Diego Velázquez, who had sent him on a mission of exploration, not of conquest.

Before leaving to do battle with Narváez, Cortés left Pedro de Alvarado in charge of the city. When Cortés told Malinalli that they had to leave the city to go fight Pánfilo de Narváez, she was very upset. Many times in her life she had had to abandon what she most cared for and loved, forced again to start from nothing to create a new world, abandoning all to gain all. But on reaching Tenochtitlán she had thought her pilgrimage had ended, that finally she could spread her roots, just like that, calmly, without noise or commotion. In peace. She did not count on things becoming complicated in unimaginable ways.

Cortés left Tenochtitlán headed for Cempoallan, where Narváez had established camp. On arriving there, he found out that Narváez was taking cover in the great temple of that city. Since Cortés knew the place well, he decided to attack at night, when he was least expected. A tropical storm appeared to change his plans, but in fact the opposite occurred. He decided to attack like the rain, unexpected and untimely. He sent eighty men into the great temple and left the rest of his army, Malinalli, the horses, and provisions on the outskirts of Cempoallan.

For Malinalli, it was a tempestuous night, by all accounts. That day she had begun to menstruate. The horses sensed it and were restless. She had to move far away from them and the men to wash her bloodstained clothes so that the horses would not become anxious. Malinalli thought that it was more likely that the Moon and not the Sun fed on blood, the blood of menstruating women, because she had noticed that each time that she menstruated the Moon was full, and so she discovered the lunar cycle was exactly the same as the menstruating cycle. The light of the Moon spread the blood in her intimate spaces. The light of the Moon—the light that would shine over victory or tragedy that night, abundance or defeat, ecstasy or death; the silver light that controlled the seas, that brought to life all the liquids in the body so that they could sing a bloody hymn to the beginning of new life, to regenerate her—this was the only one that could become her ally.

She offered her blood to the Moon, so that this night she would be with Cortés, despite the fact that she was hidden behind gray clouds. Malinalli did not want to think about what would happen to her if he was defeated. And so it seemed that the Moon had listened to her and received her offer; had contemplated the ecstasy of her liquids and responded favorably. That May night, Cortés caught Narváez by surprise and defeated him soundly even though his combined forces were less than three hundred men against the eight hundred commanded by Narváez, the majority of whom, after the battle, allied themselves with Cortés, amazed by the stories that they heard about Tenochtitlán, where there was gold for everyone.

But Cortés did not have time to celebrate his victory, for he received news that there was a Mexica uprising in Tenochtitlán, in response to a massacre conducted by Pedro de Alvarado in the great temple.

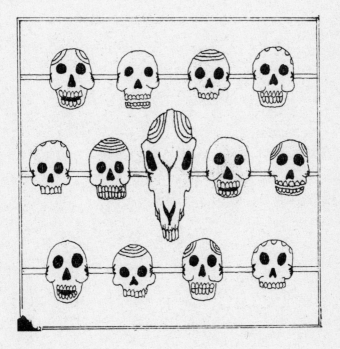

SEVEN

After that night and for many nights later, Malinalli could not sleep. She was tormented by the images of a massacre that she had not seen. Ever since she was a girl she had developed a technique for falling asleep, which consisted of closing her eyes and painting a codex in her mind. When faces, figures, glyphs, signs began to appear in her mind, she knew that she was already in the land of dreams, in the fantastic universe that belonged to her alone. That place was where she came upon her most luminous thoughts, but also her most horrifying ones.

After listening to the story about what had happened in Tenochtitlán in her absence, images came into her head as soon as she shut her eyes. Heads, legs, arms, noses, and ears flying through the air. Although she had not witnessed the killings in the Great Temple, she had Cholula as a precedent, so with utmost clarity her mind reproduced the sounds of flesh tearing, the screaming, the weeping, the explosion of harquebuses, the sound of bells on the ankles of fleeing people trying to scale the walls. Malinalli felt a shuddering in the center of her body and she opened her eyes. This would happen various times until, exhausted, she would be conquered by sleep.

Then came the worst part. A repeating dream imprisoned her mind. At the beginning of the nightmare, Malinalli was a butterfly held aloft by the wind, who observed the dancing Mexica nobles and warriors from high above. She saw how they gave themselves to the dance, concentrating, entering a state of religious exaltation. From the center of the circle in which they danced, a pillar of light rose and united the sky with the earth and cast a powerful yellow light over the dancers, who were adorned in their finest costumes, their finest feathers, their finest hides. But suddenly, a shower of bullets fell over them, piercing their chests, and their bleeding hearts turned into stone and rose to the heavens. In her nightmare, Malinalli spoke.

"Hearts of stone can also fly."

On saying this, a fascinating and terrifying image captured her attention. The stone carving of the mutilated body of the goddess Coyolxauhqui—who was sister to the god Huitzilopochtli, and who had died torn to pieces when she tried to prevent the birth of her brother from the womb of his mother, Coatlicue—came to life. She abandoned her stillness to bring together her mutilated parts; the fragments of the legs and the arms that had been separated reunited with the torso and the stone turned to flesh and the sculpture became a living thing.

"When stone turns to flesh, the heart turns to stone."

As if Malinalli had called them, some of the hearts of stone approached her face and burst into a thousand pieces, spitting streams of blood; others fell like hail and pummeled Montezuma, burying him. Malinalli's butterfly wings were bathed in blood and became heavy. Unable to fly, she fell noisily to the ground. Malinalli, having then turned into one of the dancers, tried to flee from the shotguns and the shower of stone hearts, stepping over the dismembered to scale the walls, but the blood dripping from the stones made that impossible. Her feet and hands slipped and made her fall. At that moment, she wanted to scream, to plead to heaven for help, but no voice came from her throat. Turning her face, she saw a rain of stone hearts fall on Montezuma until he was buried under them, and then a rain of swords was directed at Malinalli's chest, piercing her heart in countless spots, from which beautiful bloody feathers emerged. At this point, Malinalli opened her eyes, out of breath and full of tears.

It did no good to open her eyes. The nightmare continued. Malinalli walked without walking, saw without seeing, spoke without speaking, was there and was not there. She lived through the dramatic events of the killings without having seen them, heard them, or registered them in her memory. She had no space in her mind for the present because the images of the past, images of horror, took up all the room.

She experienced the return to Tenochtitlán as in a dream. They returned through Lake Texcoco, their canoe sliding smoothly through its waters. This time there was no welcome, no escort of nobles awaiting them, for the majority of them were dead. It had been a month since the massacre in the Great Temple and the smell of death still lingered in the air. As they made their way into the city, Malinalli's heartbeat grew faster as sorrow ran through her veins. To calm herself, she closed her eyes and tried to think of nothing. She did not want to see the signs of the calamity.

When they arrived at the place of Axayácatl, Cortés went directly to Pedro de Alvarado to ask for explanations. He had left him in charge because he had thought that he would be able to handle the Tenochans, who looked on him as a representation of Tonatiuh, the God of the Sun. When they addressed him they did not use his name but instead called him "Sun." Cortés had not counted on the fact that the responsibility he entrusted the man with would be more than he could handle. The fear of losing control had caused him to organize the massacre.

It was true that ever since the Spaniards arrived, the proud Tenochans looked on them with suspicion. They did not understand the actions of their governor Montezuma. As a ruler, he had distinguished himself for his valor, his wisdom, his intense religiosity, and his firm hand in controlling the empire. Confronted with the Spaniards, however, he proved to be weak and submissive, which did not cease to amaze the Tenochans. People in the street asked themselves if Montezuma had lost his mind, if Tenochtitlán was without a head, without a leader. It did not take long for a resistance movement to arise, headed by the lords Cacama of Tezcoco, Cuitláhuac of Iztapalapa, and Cuauhtémoc, Ahuizotl's son. From this perspective, it seemed logical that Pedro de Alvarado, fearing an insurrection that he could not control with the few men that he had been left with, decided to murder the finest warriors and most distinguished nobles who had participated in the celebrations.

The massacre provoked the feared insurrection. Cortés asked Montezuma to speak to his people from the roof garden of his palace to pacify them, but the governor was not well received by the people. The Tenochans, enraged, hurled insults and stones at him. Montezuma was hit three times. The Spanish said that this had been the cause of his death, but according to the testimony of the natives, he was assassinated by the Spaniards themselves.

Malinalli did not enter the game of explanations. She did not say anything. The effect of having been the last one to have looked into the emperor's eyes before they took him to his quarters kept her living in a time that wasn't the present. She asked herself if her nightmare was part of reality or reality part of her nightmare. And where was she anyway? Without knowing it, she saw how the Mexicas elected Cuitláhuac, Montezuma's brother, as the new emperor, who immediately organized his people to confront Cortés and his men. He did it so well that he forced the Spanish to initiate a retreat. They decided to flee at night, when the city was peaceful, so that they could take with them all the treasures that they had accumulated.

The only time that Malinalli reacted and placed herself in the present moment was when they were fleeing. The Tenochans were chasing them. One of their arrows wounded the horse that had always been her ally, the one who had been with her during the baptism, at the massacre in Cholula, in the battle against Pánfilo de Narváez; her eternal and unconditional friend. When Malinalli saw him fall wounded, time stopped. The sounds of the battle froze in the air. She could not hear anything. Everything that surrounded her disappeared from her field of vision. Only the horse existed, only the horse was dying. Malinalli felt a profound sorrow. She did not want to leave him there fallen and suffering. She embraced him and in his eyes saw fear, pain, suffering. Immediately it brought to mind Montezuma's eyes after he had been wounded by the stones. There was kindness in those eyes. There was greatness. There was elegance. Malinalli forcefully grabbed the cudgel she was using to fight the Tenochans and delivered a mortal blow to the horse's head. Then she pulled out a blade and in a fit of madness cut off its head. She wanted to take it with her, to honor it as it deserved. She did not want it to be a feast for worms. She was so wound up in her task, that she lost sight that she was still fleeing, that the battle continued, that her life was in danger. Juan Jaramillo was the one who noticed a Tenochan grab Malinalli by the hair, about to behead her. Jaramillo fired his harquebus and killed him, then ran and took hold of Malinalli, who was still cutting the horse's head off, and dragged her to the outskirts of the city, where they sat to lament their defeat. Malinalli, again absent, remained with her head on the shoulder offered by Jaramillo. He had displayed great strength and courage that night. Malinalli regretted not having made off with the horse's head; Cortés, with all of his treasures.

The defeated Cortés took up refuge in Tlaxcala, where he recovered and gathered his strength. Meanwhile, an epidemic of smallpox, brought over by the Cuban slaves that had arrived with the Spanish, ravaged the people. One of the victims was the emperor Cuitláhuac himself, who perished from it.

Then Montezuma's cousin, the young Cuauhtémoc, took the throne. One of his first actions was to order the execution of six of Montezuma's sons who were attempting to yield to the Spaniards. In spite of the epidemic, he gave orders and took measures for the defense of the city. He knew that Cortés, supported by the Tlaxcaltecans, was preparing a new invasion of Tenochtitlán.

Cortés had thirteen ships built to seize the city from the lakes surrounding it. Warriors from Cholula, Huexotzingo, and Chalco joined him. According to his calculations he would be able to bring together more than seventy-five thousand men.

Cuauhtémoc confronted the Spaniards by attacking them from the rooftops as they passed through the streets. Cortés ordered all houses destroyed, and so began the devastation of the city.

In one of his campaigns, Cortés was able to reach the

Great Temple, but the Mexicas attacked him from the rear and were able to capture more than fifty Spanish soldiers. That night, from their camp, the Spaniards heard the hymn of triumph, and knew that the captured soldiers had been sacrificed in the Great Temple itself.

Cortés decided to lay siege to the city, taking hold of the roads that connected it to the mainland, while controlling access by water with the ships and canoes of his allies. At the same time, he had the aqueducts of Chapultepec, which provided Tenochtitlán with fresh water, destroyed. He intended to make them surrender from thirst and hunger.

⊰⊹⊱

The Tenochans resisted in Tlatelolco. It was in the market, in the heart of the empire, that the final blow was dealt to the people of Tenochtitlán. There had been so many deaths from smallpox and hunger that the Spanish were finally able to overcome them. The day of the fall, they killed and captured over forty thousand natives, amid a loud chorus of screaming and weeping.

Cuauhtémoc tried to flee, but was captured and brought before Cortés.

"Lord Malinche," he said when in his presence, "I have done my duty in defense of my city and vassals and I cannot go on. So I come by force, a prisoner before your person and power. Take that knife from your belt and kill me with it."

Cortés did not kill him, but instead took him prisoner, having his feet burned until he would reveal where the gold was hidden, the gold that his troops had lost during their flight on the Sorrowful Night.

When Cortés went to Hibueras, he took the emperor with him. A Tlatelolcan in the expedition accused Cuauhtémoc of planning an insurrection against Cortés. Cortés then, after having christened the emperor with the name Fernando, ordered that he be hanged from a great ceiba, the sacred tree of the Mayans, in a place near Tabasco.

⊰⊱

There was no wind. The sun was hidden behind thick gloomy gray clouds, appearing like a dull, weak moon that struggled to remain in the sky behind the smoke that rose from the funeral pyres. It could be stared at without its rays causing harm. It had lost its brilliance and with that, the ability to see its reflection in the lakes and canals of the Valley of Anáhuac, whose dark turbid waters were soiled with blood.

The zoological garden in Montezuma's palace was empty. There were no animals. Nothing was left of the beauty and elegance of the empire.

In the ovens, the countless customary dishes for Montezuma were no longer being cooked.

The craftsmen who made jewels and clothes for the emperor were dead or had fled.

The silence was interrupted by the cries, the weeping of Cihuacóatl/Tonantzin, the snake woman known as "Our Mother."

And the fate of Cuauhtémoc passed in a whisper from mouth to mouth.

"Today our sun has been concealed; our sun has gone hiding and left us in complete darkness. We know that one day it will again shine over us. But as long as it remains hidden there in Mictlán, we should join together during this long night of this our sun of consciousness, which is the fifth sun, and we will do so by concealing in our hearts all that is dear to us: our way of speaking and rearing our children, our way of organizing and coexisting, and in so doing come to the aid of one another.

"We will conceal our Teocaltin (temples), our Calmecameh

(schools of higher learning), our Tlachcohuan (ball games), our Telpochcaltin (schools for the young), and our Cuicacaltin (hymn houses), and leave the streets deserted to lock ourselves in our homes.

"From this day forth, our homes will be our Teocaltin, our Calmecameh, our Tlachcohuan, our Telpochcaltin, and our Cuicacaltin.

"From this day forth, until the day the new sun rises, the fathers and mothers will be the teachers and guides who while they live will lead their children by the hand. May the fathers and mothers never forget to tell their children what the Anáhuac has been to this day, under the protection of the Lord of All Things, our Lord Ometeotl-Ometecuhtli, and resulting from the customs and teachings that our elders instilled in our parents, and that with such great effort they in turn instilled in us. Also never forget to tell your children what one day this Anáhuac will be again; that after this long night the sixth sun, the sun of justice, will rise."

Malinalli asked herself what she had done wrong. Where had she failed? Why hadn't she been granted the privilege of helping her people? Just as Cortés had been the answer to Montezuma's fears, and the gold obtained, to Cortés's ambition, she wanted to know what end was fulfilled by Tenochtitlán's destruction. The wishes of the Tlaxcaltecans? Of the gods? A necessity of the universe? To a cycle of life of death? She did not know at all. The only thing that she was certain of was that she hadn't been able to save anything.

Malinalli thought about her grandmother, about how fortunate she had been not to see the destruction of her world, her gods. Malinalli was confused. She felt guilty and responsible for what had happened. To justify herself, she thought that perhaps what was dying was not dying at all; that it was clear from the human sacrifices that the only thing that died on the stone was the body, the shell, but in exchange for the liberation of the spirit. The lives of the sacrificed belonged to the gods and to them they returned when sacrificed; the priests did not destroy anything, for the life that they freed from the prison of the body continued its destiny in the heavens in order to feed the Sun. Her emotional well-being depended on accepting all this as certain, but she did and did not agree, believed and did not believe.

If she looked around her, everything spoke of an eternal cycle of life and death. The flowers died and became fertilizer for other flowers. The fish, the birds, the plants nourished each other. Yes, but she was convinced that Quetzalcóatl had come to this world to proclaim that the gods did not feed on the blood of the sacrificed, but rather, on their thoughts and intentions. That the dream of mankind was the apprenticeship of the gods and the apprenticeship of mankind was the eternal thought of the gods. And that the gods fed off their own essence, from the soul they had created. This was not accomplished through physical death, but through the medium of the word. When one prayed, when one named the gods, nourished them, honored them, returned to them the life that they had given us at birth.

The warriors believed that the body is what maintains the soul prisoner. Whoever controlled the body was the owner of the spirit it sheltered. That was one of the beliefs that had worked against the Mexicas. In their first confrontations with the Spaniards, they were surprised to see that their intention was the annihilation of the enemy, and not the capture. Their own great forces of war functioned in completely the opposite way. The Mexicas believed that a good warrior should capture the enemy. If he did so, he became a sort of god, for the control of the body gave him access to the control of the spirit. That is why they did not kill in the battlefield, but took prisoners. If they killed their enemies, they immediately liberated the spirit and that was a defeat, not a victory. Capturing them to later sacrifice them before their gods was what gave their deaths meaning.

Malinalli agreed only in the sense that life was defended not by struggling to save a body from death, but its spirit. Only if the idea of death did not exist, could she understand eternity, and from that perspective she had not acted wrongly. The only thing she had wanted was to save the spirit of Quetzalcóatl, which the Mexicas had kept imprisoned for so long through the practice of human sacrifices; to free it from its captors and allow it to purify itself and be reborn to men, completely renewed. But who was she for such lofty ambitions? Could she really decide what should live and what should die? At least she was sure that in her own self she could, and there Quetzalcóatl's spirit was more alive than ever. The Spaniards could not destroy it because they could not even perceive it. They had only destroyed what they could see and touch. The rest was intact.

⊰⊱

Malinalli embroidered feathers on a cape she had made for her son, with feathers that she had saved from the palace of Montezuma; with cotton that she had found in what had been the market of Tlatelolco; with jade stones and sea shells that Cortés had given her because for him they held no value. It was a cape for a prince. That's how Malinalli wanted him to appear on the day of his baptism. He had been born a week before, in a house in Coyoacán, where she lived with Cortés. She gave birth to him as her mother had given birth to her, squatting. Except that she did not have a bathhouse, or a midwife, or a burial for the umbilical cord in the field of battle so that the boy would become a warrior. That was fine with Malinalli. She did not want her son to kill. She was tired of the dead. Cortés's eyes were also sick of looking at death, so many mutilated bodies, so much destruction. His arms were tired of taking up the sword, of cutting, of severing. That is why, months before, they had gone to live in Coyoacán and seek rest. They both yearned to rest.

Nevertheless, Cortés was not a man who could live in repose. If he was not planning strategies of attack or defense, he felt as if time was getting away from him. The worst was that when he had time to think on his own, feelings of guilt assaulted him. He did not know if it had been the right thing to demolish so many pyramids, burn so many codices. His justification was that there had been no choice, that he had done it defending life, but sometimes he asked himself for what. Before him he had the opportunity to create everything anew. He had destroyed everything to create everything. But what? He could design plans for new cities, distribute lands, approve laws, but deep down—very deep down—he knew that life continued to be a mystery. It didn't belong to him. He could destroy it but not create it. That made all the difference. In other words, he was not a god.

Suddenly he had been overcome with the desire to create a life and had sought out Malinalli to do it.

When Malinalli became pregnant she felt complete, happy. She knew that in her womb there was beating the heart of a being that would unite two worlds. The blood of Moors and Christians with that of the Indians, that pure, unmixed race.

During her pregnancy, when she did not know whether she would have a boy or a girl, she wove blankets from *malinalli* fiber in a loom. Malinalli braided *malinalli*. The "Braided Grass" prepared the warp of her fabric, weaving the grass. She was going to dress her child with all her being. She was going to cover it like the shell that covers the seed in order to reverse the process taking place in her womb. Malinalli knew that just as every plant fulfilled the cycle of being sown, sprouting, flowering, and death, always going from darkness toward the light, likewise within her a seed was germinating that would come out into the light. The seed of a plant, in order to germinate, had to cast off the shell that was covering it. She wondered if that was why priests who sacrificed prisoners flayed them and then wore their skin. The seed loses everything to gain everything. It loses its shell to become a plant, which is in turn everything, earth, water, sun, and wind. But when her child came out of the womb, she wanted to continue to cover it and that is why she made blankets of *malinalli*.

When the boy was born, Cortés celebrated for three days. It was his firstborn, a male child. Now he had an heir, someone to perpetuate his name. But a black thought tarnished his joy, that his son was a son born outside of wedlock, and moreover, from a slave. His son would not be well looked upon in the court of Spain. His son was a mestizo. To complicate matters, his wife, Catalina Xuárez, had arrived in Mexico. From the very first day, she made great effort to ruin whatever satisfaction remained in Cortés.

Catalina had not been able to give him children and was terribly jealous of Malinalli and her child. Cortés, attempting to please her, organized a welcoming party. During the feast, Catalina pursued Cortés everywhere, not to enjoy his company, but to argue. The quarrel grew so loud that most of the guests decided to leave early. Cortés and Catalina continued arguing in their bedroom.

The day after, while Malinalli nursed her son, she was told by one of the servants that Catalina had been found dead that morning. A servant woman had found her in bed, dressed in the same clothes that she had worn to the party. There were bruises on her neck. Her pearl necklace had been torn off and the bed urinated on. The rumor of a possible murder spread all over.

One of the things that most affected Malinalli was that the necklace had been torn off. Someone had disconnected Catalina from the necklace of creation.

⊰◈⊱

The starry infinite night watched over Cortés and Malinalli. They were sitting around a bonfire, surrounded by soldiers who ate in silence. In the field, there were various fires that were reflected in the stars. Malinalli watched Cortés, who was looking all around, now at the sky, now at the fire, now at the ground. From the day that she had watched him cleaning his weapons and sharpening his sword, she knew that an obsidian wind was threatening her. She knew perfectly well how he was the father of her son, how his blood had been re-created in her entrails. She thought that she had always known him; he was so familiar, so near, that she accepted him as part of her destiny, as if he had been born from her own womb, as if he had been born to listen to her tongue, as if he had been born to injure her heart. On noticing Cortés's restless gazing, she easily discovered in it a permanent dissatisfaction, a constant disappointment, as if the only thing that could bring him satisfaction and pleasure was the act of conquering. Not the goals achieved. Not the victories. Not the infinite power he possessed.

"This man is insatiable," she told herself. "It seems that the only thing that awakens him to life is death. The only thing that gives him joy is blood, the urge to destroy, to break apart, to tear, to transform."

She felt pity for him and for the first time had compassion

for this obsessive and terrible man. She felt it a shame that he could not be at peace. They were on the way to Hibueras, with plans of conquest, and Malinalli was afraid that if he was successful his desire for conquest would grow and he would go mad wanting more and more. She imagined that there would never be any rest.

"What a dreadful punishment!" she thought. "For this man is the father of my child."

On their way to Hibueras, they passed by the place where Malinalli was born. To walk again on the ground where she had played so often with her grandmother, where she had known the unconditional love that she offered, was a strange experience. Everything seemed diminished, made smaller. What in the memories of her childhood was enormous, was there, but now she saw it in its proper dimensions.

She had contemplated this return many times, but had never made it. It was not until then, in the company of Cortés, that she retraced her past steps. Some distance before arriving, Malinalli's heart was already uneasy, burning with its beating. The blood pulsed in her eyes and her look displayed the innocence of a girl and the endless hatred of one who for years had held on to a grief, who for years had kept a latent anxiety concealed deep in her heart, a forgotten ache that awoke hastily as Malinalli approached the place where she had been abandoned by her mother.

She could suddenly feel, in every pore of her body, all the grief of her infancy. "Destiny is exact and what is written in the stars is fulfilled," were the words that Malinalli remembered at the moment that she saw her mother anew. There, standing before her, was that phantom that had loomed so frequently in her memory, but with a different appearance. There was the grandiose image of her mother, so strong and powerful, now appearing agonized, withered, worn out, and full of sorrow, wearing a mask of humility. By her side was Malinalli's brother. She saw herself in the mirror of his gaze and recognized immediately the sensibility and inner world of a man who appeared to her as something long yearned for. He was so like her, so like her in face, in his heartbeat, in his breathing. It was as if she saw herself turned into a man. When he saw her, he immediately smiled. Malinalli's heart beat with a deafening force. Her eyes were about to burst with tears. The feeling was similar to the first time she had fallen in love, the first time she had cared for someone. She wanted to kiss him, to embrace him, to caress him. But she was able to control herself, and returned his greeting with another smile. This world of perceptions of silent dialogues, of looks and gestures, was broken by Malinalli's mother.

"My daughter, what a pleasure to see you!" she said, as she extended her hand to touch her, to caress her face. Malinalli eluded the contact.

"I am not your daughter nor do I consider you my mother," she said. "You offered me no caress or loving word, no kind gesture or world of protection on that day when with such exact and punctual cruelty you gave me away. That day you decided that I would be a slave, you took away my heart's freedom and my mind's imagination."

Malinalli's mother could not hold it in anymore and her eyes spilled copious tears. Her dry lips pronounced words whose sound could move stones, and the most hardened hearts.

"My daughter, Malinalli, by the great expanse of the seas, by the power of the stars, by the rain that washes and renews all, forgive me. I was guided by desire, blinded by life, attracted to what breathed. I could no longer be married to death. Your father had died, was inert, no word came out of his mouth nor light from his eyes. I could not stay bound to his immobility. I was still a young woman and wanted to live, I wanted to feel. Forgive me, for I ignored the fact that your child's heart could suffer. I thought that, being so young, you would have no memory of me, that you wouldn't know that I had given you away. And I imagined that your grandmother would make you strong, that she would open your eyes, that she would look after your heart and your thoughts. I abandoned you to be myself. Forgive me."

Malinalli was moved, her heart disturbed. She was about to embrace her mother and heal her wounds, but she held herself back. Her rancor, the pain of abandonment, was more powerful than her mother's plea. Containing her emotions and in a display of cruelty, she responded with a coldness sharper than ice.

"I don't have anything to forgive you for. I can't forgive that which made my fate better than yours. You gave me away, but fortune gave me power and riches. I am the woman of the foremost man, the woman of the man who is the new world. You stayed here in the old, in the dust, in what no longer exists. I, on the other hand, am the new city, the new beliefs, the new culture. I invented the world in which you are now standing. Don't worry, in my codices you don't exist. I erased you long ago."

The mother pleaded again.

"The punishment that you grant me is small. I accept that my abandonment was more violent than your words, but, for the time that you and I were one life, for the time that inside my womb you were nourished, for the time that my eyes were your eyes and my hands your touch, I dare to beg of you to have mercy on us, not to do violence to our bodies, to spare our lives, to grant us life, lady of the new world."

"Your fear surprises me. I see that you are unaware that

to die is not to end, it is to continue, to evolve. Look at me! I survived the death that you had decided for me. It was you who invented all the punishments that you now suffer from. It was you who made the prison where you now live; but settle down, be calm, all rancor was expelled from me the moment that I saw you again. I have no wish to harm you. Be at peace. I will not hurt you, not you, nor my brother. I will forget everything and let my resentment be cast out into nothingness."

With rage and with beauty, Malinalli tore her eyes away from her mother's gaze and returned them again to her brother. Her face softened and her eyes, full of tenderness, kissed the face of her lost brother. She returned his smile with kindness and then continued on her way.

All paths change us. After a while of walking, Malinalli was able to undo the image of her mother that she had kept in her heart for years. With each step, the certainty of the abandonment faded little by little, and after a while Malinalli could feel love for her mother. When she was far from her she could love her and look upon her with different eyes.

She was ashamed of the disrespect, the arrogance, the disdain with which she had treated her progenitor. Now she felt tenderness. In her heart, she forgave her and at that moment remembered anxiously that she too had abandoned her son, that she had left him without her warmth, her breast, her lips, her gaze. She remembered the face of her son, barely a year old, grabbing her legs, begging her without words not to abandon him, begging her with smiles to stay near him. She remembered his cries when he was taken from her arms. She remembered what his life had felt like inside her and his lips on her nipples. The memories became one with the tears and she felt compassion for her mother. How had she dared accuse, when she too had been capable of abandoning!

She blamed herself for going against his wishes simply because she had wanted to stay by the side of that man who awoke in her the greatest of lusts: the longing for power, the desire to be different, unique, and special. She felt shame and a profound ache that ran through her spinal cord. The chill of suffering got inside her bones, became unbearable. She didn't forgive herself, didn't give herself the satisfaction, didn't pity herself. From that moment on, the memory of her son would not leave her. The memory of the abandonment would be a nightmare in her mind, a hell in the palm of her hand, a mania in her look. She despised herself, and felt disdain in her heart and hatred, infinite hatred for Cortés. Disgust, emptiness, anxiety and bitterness, an uncontrollable urge to stone Cortés's face, to destroy his image, burn his thoughts, undo him, bring him down, seeing him in pieces in the wind.

She went to meet him and told him to follow her, that she had something important to tell him. Cortés obeyed, convinced that she was going to tell him about some secret plan or some intrigue against him. He followed her in silence until they reached a high spot in a wood. From there, the infinitely green tropical jungles could be seen, and one could understand the beauty of all things. Cortés confronted Malinalli.

"We are here," he said. "So now tell me, what is it that you want?"

"What I want, I can't touch. It is far away from me. What I want is to feel the skin of our son. What I want is to fill his thoughts with beautiful words. What I want is to protect his dreams, to make him feel that the world is a safe place, that death will be far away from him, that he and I are one, that we are united by a force greater than our wills. What I want I can't have because you drag me down the path of your obsessions. You promised me freedom and have not given it to me. Because of you, I don't have a soul or a heart. I am a chattering object that you use without feeling for the sake of your conquests. I am the beast of burden of your desires, your whims, your madness. What I want is for you to stop your thoughts and for a moment realize that you are in the midst of life. And that those around you also breathe, blood also runs through our veins, and we feel loved or hurt; that we are not stone, or scraps of wood, or iron utensils. We are flesh, feeling, and thought. We are as you yourself say: verb incarnate, word in flesh. What I want is for you to awake and accept the opportunity I am offering you to be happy, to be a family, to be one being. I offer you the kisses of the stars, the embrace of the sun and the moon. Forget this absurd idea of going to conquer Hibueras, please, Hernán, banish such madness from your mind. Stop the interminable insanity in your heart and drink peace to quench your ambition and your delirium. That is want I want, and it is in your hands to give it to me."

Cortés gave her a strange look. He was moved. No one had ever talked to him with so much truth, and yes, in reality that is what he too wanted in the profundity of his being, in the reality of his soul, but he couldn't accept it. He could not reject the destiny of becoming the greatest of all men, the most powerful, the most immense, in exchange for a city and a woman already conquered. Because of this, he changed his mind right away and looked at Malinalli as if she were a mad and stupid woman who truly only served him as an object, as an instrument of conquest.

"Be reasonable, Marina," he laughed and said. "Don't let your feelings poison the meaning of our lives and accept that your mission is simply to be my 'Tongue.' Do not interrupt my thoughts again with your foolishness. And don't think about repeating such stupid laments. Don't waste my time. Dedicate yourself to obeying and be grateful for what I have done for you, because it is bigger than your life!"

After having said this, he moved away from her and toward camp, his irritation intense. Then, as if nature were confederate with Malinalli's feelings, as if nature understood the justness of her words, the wind blew in a supernatural fashion, night fell instantly, the clouds covered the sun and the rain became indistinguishable from her tears.

❖

That night Cortés got drunk. He drank to escape from himself, to flee from the words that Malinalli had pronounced hours before. To flee from the truth. He did not want to hear that a man is a transitory thing in this life, that no one remains forever on the earth, that power is fleeting, that time lays waste to all. Delirious, he sang and his off-key voice shattered the beauty of a song, or he recited verses in Latin, or pieces of poems that made no sense. The alcohol changed his behavior completely. Suddenly, his attitude changed. From raucous joy he went to anger, to violence.

"No one," he screamed. "Listen to me! No one will ever betray me again. None of my men will be able to turn against me. No one will plan intrigues regarding my person, because whoever does, whoever dares, will die in an embarrassing and cruel manner. No one will be allowed to oppose my thoughts, my will. No one will be allowed to contradict my ideas, or ever to divert my intuitions. Those who are near me, who know me, have to be a shadow of my person, for only then will I be able to achieve all my goals, only then, can the infinite power of my emotions reach its joyful destiny. Everyone listen! Because if I die, so will you."

At that instant, he kept his eyes on Malinalli, who was watching Cortés's transformation and insanity. In those moments, he was truly frightening; he was someone who had lost control, was frenzied. It seemed as if his mind was set on fire with each gulp of alcohol he drank. It ravaged his blood, and he became possessed by a desire for greatness and an unknown vengeance that seemed to come from some errant genes that forced him to transform the world into an arena of combat and death. That feeling of vengeance and anger was encrusted in Cortés's heart and blood, as if his rancor caused a festering wound that affected all his thoughts.

Malinalli grew afraid and was overcome with a feeling of despair. Alcohol was a bad companion to men and to the gods. It had changed Quetzalcóatl in such a fashion that he had been capable of fornicating with his sister, and it was said that Cortés, under the influence of alcohol, had strangled his wife. This man was capable of the basest murder! A tragic omen coursed through her blood and warned her of her own danger, but at the same time offered her the serenity to feign calm in the heat of battle. Cortés pulled her toward him and said in a low voice:

"So you no longer want to be a slave, is that so? Then I will do as you please, I am going to make you into a wife, but not *my* wife. You are close to me, but we will not be united. Your blood and my blood created a new blood that belongs to both of us, but now, your blood will mix with someone else's. I will continue to be your lord but you will never be my wife."

Then an extraordinary scream came from Cortés's throat.

"Jaramiloooooo! Come here, my faithful soldier."

Jaramillo obeyed and when he was next to him, Cortés took his hand and placed it on Malinalli's heart. Jaramillo, embarrassed, tried to pull it away, but Cortés held it firmly in place.

"Approach this woman," he said. "Feel her heart, her touch, her hair, because from here on, she is yours. Take this woman to sate all your desires in her and to see if you can become me." He laughed in an exaggerated and false manner.

Cortés chose Jaramillo to be with Malinalli because, aside from being one of his most valued men, he was the most trusted. He wanted to bind Malinalli to Jaramillo for two reasons: to bind Jaramillo to his will and to deal with Malinalli from a more reasonable distance, a less emotional one. In such a way he could make best use of that surprisingly intelligent woman who was indispensable to his plans.

Jaramillo gave Cortés an incredulous and surprised look. He didn't know if this was a joke, if what his superior was saying was due to drunkenness or delirium, or if he was mocking him. There was uncertainty in Jaramillo's eyes and joy in his heart. He looked away so that Cortés would not notice that Malinalli was the woman he had longed for since that long ago day, on the shores of the river, when Cortés penetrated her for the first time. That woman that he was now offering was the one that had heated his thoughts countless times, the woman that he had always wanted naked in his arms. Nonetheless, Jaramillo took Cortés apart to question him.

"Hernán, what do you mean by this? Why are you making me Marina's lord? Why this wish, suddenly risen from nowhere and without reason, that I be her husband?"

"Jaramillo, don't lie to yourself," Cortés responded. "For days, months, and years Marina has appeared in your dreams. You are already a husband since you think so insistently about her. Just as I see these stars above us, I have seen in the depth of your mind how many times you have desired her. You are my friend and I give you your wish in exchange for which you will give Marina a name, a status, and bring protection to my son. This is the biggest charge I have bestowed upon you, the greatest mission I can place in your hands. Jaramillo, help me make history."

Later, Cortés and his retinue were witnesses at the wedding of Jaramillo and Malinalli. On the night of the wedding, Jaramillo, by then already drunk and full of desire, penetrated her again and again. He drank from her breasts, kissed her skin, submerged himself in her, emptied all his being in Malinalli, and fell asleep.

Cortés, completely inebriated, slept spread-eagled. He looked half dead, like someone still oblivious to the fact that he had torn away the best part of himself. The only one who was awake was Malinalli. The desire to set herself on fire kept her alert, the desire to evaporate, to become a star, to melt into the sun, just as Quetzalcóatl had done. She longed to stop being herself, to fly, to be a part of everything and nothing, not to see, or hear, or feel, or know, but, above all, not to remember. She felt humiliated, sad, alone, and she could not figure how to let out the frustration from her being, how to cast her grief to the wind, how to change her decision to be present in this world.

She thought of the moments in which Cortés's mouth and her mouth had been one mouth only, and the thought of Cortés and his tongue one single idea, one new universe. The tongue had joined them and the tongue had separated them. The tongue was the cause of everything. Malinalli had destroyed Montezuma's empire with her tongue. Thanks to her words, Cortés had made allies that ensured his conquest. She decided then to punish the instrument that had created that universe. At night, she crossed through the jungle until she found an agave plant from which she pulled a thorn and with it, pierced her tongue. She spat blood as if she were ridding her mind of a poison, her body of shame, and her heart of its wound. After that night, her tongue would never be the same. It would not create marvels in the sky or worlds in the ears. It would never again be the instrument of any conquest, nor order thought, nor explain history. Her tongue was bifurcated and broken, it was no longer an instrument of the mind. As a result, the expedition to Hibueras was a failure. Cortés's defeat was buried in silence. Reality saw them return vanquished.

❈❈❈

In the ship that brought them back from Hibueras, silence reigned. From the gunwale Malinalli watched the sea, its constant movement, its colors. The thought occurred to her that the sea was the best image of god, because it seemed infinite, because her eyes could not take it all in.

Malinalli was about to be a mother for the second time. Her heart guarded a silence and in that silence all the sounds of the world were evident. To feel a life within her life deeply affected Malinalli's heart. Not only did she bring with her a piece of flesh in her flesh but she shared her soul with its soul. And perhaps, as these two souls joined, all souls were, and a heaven of souls was perhaps like a heaven of stars. A few days afterward, as Malinalli gazed at the stars, she was surprised by contractions and gave birth squatting on the deck of the ship. Her daughter came out covered in blood and in the light of the stars. Malinalli remembered that Marina, her mestizo name, the one with which Cortés had baptized her, meant she who comes from the sea. The sea, "el mar," was also contained within the name of her son Martín. Her daughter, since she came from the womb of the sea, was also water from her water. She decided to return her daughter's umbilical cord to the sea, to the broken vessel of the universe, from which all beings had come. She felt great relief when the umbilical cord came loose from her fingers and crashed into the salty waters. For a few moments it floated on the surface and then it was embraced and brought down into the deep dark waters. For some strange reason she understood that eternity was an instant, an instant of peace where everything is understood, everything makes sense, even if it could not be explained in words, for there was no language to name it. With her tongue paralyzed by emotion, Malinalli took her small daughter and offered her breast to her so that she might drink milk, drink the sea, so that she might feed from love, poetry, the light of the moon, and so doing she understood that her daughter should be called María. María, like the Virgin. In María she would renew herself.

She didn't hesitate in responding to Jaramillo, her husband, who had asked her if it was true that women who nursed died a little.

"No, they are reborn," she said categorically.

Jaramillo also liked the name of María for his daughter. He remembered that when he was a child he had helped during the funeral of a woman close to the family. The adults were so busy that they didn't notice when Jaramillo approached her to look at her. His child's sensibility was deeply affected by the tranquillity and stillness of the woman. On looking at her face without a soul, he understood that death was a necessary act and it filled him with terror. He did not want what he loved to die. Despairing, he sought aid and his eyes found a wooden sculpture of the Virgin Mary with a naked child in her arms. The child Jaramillo asked her silently:

"Why is it that whatever gives life, must die?"

He got no answer, but ever since, he was very moved when looking at a dead woman or a woman nursing.

Jaramillo tenderly kissed his daughter's brow and caressed his wife's face. Malinalli remembered the moment that Cortés had wedded her to him, and it was no longer a bitter memory. What's more, she felt tenderness for Hernán, that little man who wanted to be as immense as the sea. In the depth of her being she was very grateful to him for marrying her to Jaramillo. He was a good man, respectful, loving, brave, and loyal. And finally, Cortés had done her a favor by distancing her from his side. Her marriage had perhaps saved her from death, because she, like many others, also suspected that Cortés had murdered his wife, that it hadn't been an accident, that she hadn't died naturally, and that, one way or another, if she had married him, Cortés inevitably, for some hidden reason, would have killed her. This man not only conquered, but murdered what he loved. He killed his women so that they would be his alone. She had to face the fact then that Cortés loved her, not as she would have wanted it, but that he loved her. If not, he would not have given her part of her freedom or respected her life. Although, thinking it over, perhaps it was not love but convenience. The truth was that Cortés needed her by his side as translator.

"What is it that joined me with the abyss of this man?" Malinalli asked herself silently. "Where did the stars interweave our history? Who wove the thread of our lives? How is it that my god and his god could speak and design our union? A child of his blood was born from my womb and a daughter from the will of his whim was also born of my womb. He chose the man who would insert his seed in my flesh, not me. But I am grateful to him. I had no eyes to look on anyone who was not him and by forcing me, he made me discover a man who always had been watchful of me, of my eyes, my body, my words."

Then Malinalli became liquid, milk in her breasts, tears in her eyes, sweat on her body, saliva in her mouth, water of gratefulness.

❖

When Malinalli stepped on solid earth, the sound of her heart was a drum of anxiety that demanded from the depths of her life an embrace with her son. The embrace of a child whom she had abandoned to give herself over to the delirium of conquest of a man who set her against her own will, against her wishes, against her love, against her thoughts. An absurd conquest that had been a failure and broken her inside.

It was unforgivable to have abandoned her son when he had needed her most, when it was necessary that he identify himself with the force of her love, with the wisdom of his ancestors, with her caresses, with the silence of her gaze, where words weren't necessary. The lost silence, the absent smiles, and the empty arms pained her. Like her mother, she had abandoned what she had given birth to. The welcoming ceremonies seemed endless, the speeches that she had to translate, everything that impeded her from seeing her son immediately. When she was finally able to go look for him in the house of one of Cortés's relatives where the boy had stayed, she was afraid. A fear of seeing in the eyes of her son the same indifference with which she had looked at her own mother.

The child was playing in the patio of the house, caressed by the sun, amidst trees and puddles of water. When she saw him, Malinalli recognized him right away. He had grown. He was making mud figures, creating a fantastic universe which, painfully, she was not a part of. The child fit the same image of tenderness and beauty that Malinalli kept in her memory. The child was the same, yes, but also so different! She noticed that some of his gestures were like hers, but his manners were like his father's. Beautiful and proud. Loving and innocent. Whimsical and horrible. Full of nuances, full of colors, full of songs, such was the child she had abandoned.

She walked toward him full of love, full of tenderness, full of anxiety. She wanted to feel his skin on hers, his heart on her heart. She wanted to return to him in an instant, all her presence, all her company, erase with one stroke the months of absence, the months of abandonment.

When she embraced him, when she said his name, when she touched him, Martín looked at her as if he did not know her, as if he had never seen her, and went off running. Malinalli, in a fit of rage, of despair, of madness, ran after him, ordering him to stop, screaming that she was his mother. The boy did not stop, he continued to run as if he wanted to flee from his destiny, flee from her forever. The more his mother ran after him, the more he was afraid, and the more he was afraid, the more full of rage Malinalli became. Rage chased fear. The wound chased freedom. Guilt chased innocence. Finally, Malinalli was able stop her son by force, and doing so, without meaning to she hurt him and the boy looked at her full of panic and began to cry. His cries were so deep, as razor-edged as a sharpened knife, that they were easily able to penetrate the mantle of flesh that covered Malinalli's heart, and opened an unhealed wound, that of her own abandonment. In a great paradox, the abandoned one wounded the abandoned one with his scorn. Malinalli felt as if each caress, each attempt at love toward her son was torture, a nightmare, an injury to both of them. Then in a gesture of madness, she slapped her son so that he would calm down, so that he would not try to flee from her.

"Maltín!" she screamed in a thunderous voice. "Don't run from me!"

"I am not Maltín. I am Martín. I am not your son."

Malinalli wanted to rip out her tongue, break it, make it flexible so that it could finally pronounce the letter "r." In the pain that her child's words caused, Malinalli turned to the Náhuatl so that she would not make any mistakes, to speak from her heart.

"You have already erased me from your memory? I haven't. I have kept you in my memory all this time. You are my human creation, born from me. You are my quetzal feather, my turquoise necklace."

The boy, not understanding her well—since no one else had spoken to him in Náhuatl—but absolutely feeling all of his mother's energy, her body language and what her look said, remained paralyzed, still, silent and on looking at her recognized in the eyes of his mother his own eyes, and he cried in a different manner. He cried to retch through his eyes all the emotional poison that a four-year-old child can keep. Then he ran again, as he screamed at his mother.

"Let me go! I'm scared of you! Leave! I hate you!"

Malinalli, even more hurt, went after him again. The boy screamed desperately, "Palomaaaa! Mama, Paloma!"

The fact that her son thought of another woman as his real mother drove her crazy. Malinalli felt as if she was leaving her body. Her head was about to burst. Her heart was a war drum. The child reached the arms of the woman named Paloma and hugged her tightly. Malinalli, who had thought that she had felt the wound of love before, realized that nothing had been as painful and as hurtful as this moment that presented itself like a nightmare. Beside herself, having lost all control, she ripped the child from the arms of Paloma, even though he was kicking and swinging.

Malinalli took him by force by one of his arms and dragged him violently the whole way home.

The child cried until he grew tired, until there were no tears left in him, until his hoarse voice gave out. When her son closed his eyes, it was Malinalli's turn. She cried so much that her eyes became deformed, till she made peace with herself. Silence reigned. Malinalli looked at the light of the stars through her window, her face as innocent as when she had been four. That night, Malinalli was a girl frightened that love was not certain; she was a girl frightened that the fruit would not recognize the seed; a girl frightened to imagine that the stars disdained the sky. She turned and looked at the beautiful face of her son. For some strange reason, she remembered her father, whom she had never seen, whom she knew only in spirit. She came near him and with a timid hand caressed her son's brow. Afraid that he would wake up, she whispered.

"My tiny son, my hummingbird feather, my jade bead, my turquoise necklace, eyes lie, they make mistakes, they see things that don't exist, that are not there. My boy, look at me with your eyes closed. See me that way and you will remember me and know how much I love you. For a time I stopped looking with my eyes and I was mistaken. Only when we are children do we see the truth because our eyes are true, we speak the truth because what we feel is true. Only when we are children do we not betray ourselves, do we not deny the rhythm of the cosmos. I am only eyes that cry for your pains. When you cry, my chest tightens and my thoughts are lost in your memory. You are engraved in the bottom of my heart, with my grandmother, with my gods of stone, with the sacred songs of my ancestors. I put flesh and color in your spirit. I washed your skin with tears when you were given to me by the Lord of All Things."

The child, with his eyes closed, in that blindness that sees everything, seemed to hear her, seemed to forgive her, seemed to love her.

"If I could only feel that you love me, that you understand me, that I am not a stranger to you, that I am not what frightens you, that I am not what hurts you, I would be capable of abandoning my life, leaving everything, if with it you, my adored son, son of my blood, son of my heart, could receive my love."

Malinalli tenderly kissed her son's eyelids and sang him a beautiful lullaby in Náhuatl, the language of his ancestors. It was the same song with which hundreds of times she had put him to sleep in her arms when he was an infant. Her son's soul seemed to recognize the song and at that instant the room where he was seemed to acquire a new light. It was as if it were illuminated by a light source that came from none other than Malinalli's heart, a blue light that passed through the body of the boy, who couldn't help but feel the profound love, and even though he was asleep, he smiled and the smile said everything. For Malinalli, that smile became an instant of love much more powerful than the long months of separation. Understanding and beauty had settled in the hearts of both mother and child. Malinalli remained awake till dawn, till the first light of day grazed her son's eyelids and he awoke. When the boy looked at his mother he did not cry, but amply took her in, before falling asleep again in her lap.

Martín, like his blind great-grandmother, experienced that in the silence of the gaze is where one can truly see. For Malinalli this was a knowledge that she had acquired as a child.

In all the months that she had been apart from her son and it had been impossible for her to see him, she had imagined him much better than now as she watched him at length. Inspired by that truth that illuminates all things, she spoke to her son in Spanish. It was at that moment that she discovered the beauty of Cortés's language and appreciated that god had given her that new method with which to express herself, in a language which opened new spaces in her mind. Thanks to it, her son could understand his mother's love.

The relationship between Martín and Malinalli improved little by little, and the silver cord that nourished their union was reestablished completely.

EIGHT

The sky had tones of orange and pink. The air carried the aroma of spikenard and orange trees in bloom. Malinalli embroidered and Jaramillo, next to her, smoked. Martín and María played in the patio of the house that their parents had built together. It was a beautiful patio surrounded by a series of arches and with a fountain in each of the cardinal points. From each fountain there was a canal that carried water to the center of the patio, forming a silver cross. The patio was not only an architectural creation, a harmonious play of spaces, but it was a mythical center, a point of convergence for various spiritual traditions. It was the place where Malinalli, Jaramillo, and the children interwove the threads of their souls with the cosmos. In the water they recognized each other, they reencountered themselves. They were renewed.

"Those who are able to unravel within themselves the secret of everything become mirror people who know how to transform themselves into the Sun, the Moon, or Venus," Malinalli had told Jaramillo when, during one of their first conversations, they had discussed the design of their house. Together they decided that water would be its center.

Both were delighted by water. They liked to caress each other while one washed the body of the other with water that Malinalli had perfumed with spikenard from the garden. Sometimes, they had to interrupt the bath to kiss, to lick each other till they were exhausted, till they ended up dripping in sweat and semen and had to wash again. The bath was the ritual that first united them. For Jaramillo water was essential. He had visited the Alhambra as a child and had been fascinated by that mirror of the sky, with its interior courtyards, its canals, its fountains. He felt that God was there. When Malinalli spoke to him about Tula, another mirror of the sky, they both felt that there was something that joined them together far beyond the body, time, war, or the dead: a liquid god. The house that they designed together and built was a small Eden. Malinalli could not help but bless the Muslims who built the Alhambra and stamped in the soul of the child an indelible fingerprint. Thanks to them— among others—their house was a gift to sight, to smell, to the ear, to touch. The games of light, of shadows, the flowers and aromatic plants, the constant gurgling of water, the taste of the fruit from the garden, provided them with daily happiness. Happiness, a word that acquired meaning late in Malinalli's life, but that had finally done so.

Her heart was pleased when she watched the new shoots of corn in the field behind the house. The first harvest was obtained from the grains of corn that had come from her grandmother, which Malinalli had always kept with her. Next to the cornfield there was a garden where plants of European origin lived peacefully next to Mexican plants. Malinalli loved to create new dishes. She would try new combinations of onions, garlic, cilantro; of basil, parsley, tomatoes, cactus; of pomegranate, plantains, mangos, oranges, coffee, wheat, corn, and cacao. The new flavors in the food arose without resisting their mestizo origins. The different ingredients accepted each other without problems and the result was surprising.

It was the same result that she had achieved within her womb. Her children were the product of different bloods, different smells, different aromas, different colors. Just like the earth brought forth corn that was blue, white, red, and yellow—but allowed them to mix—it was possible to create a new race on the earth. A race that would contain them all. A race where the Giver of Life could be remade, with all manner of names and shapes. That was the race of her children.

She loved to watch them run around the patio and play in the waters of the fountains that were reminiscent of Tula and the Alhambra at once. She liked that they spoke both Náhuatl and Spanish; that they ate bread and tortillas. But it pained her that they would not see what had been the Valley of Anáhuac, what had been Tenochtitlán. The more she tried to describe it to them, the more impossible it seemed. So she decided to sketch for them a codex—her familiar codex—and teach them how to decipher its language, understand her signs. It was important that aside from learning to read Spanish, they learn how to read codices. A Mayan poem said that "those who are looking, those who are telling, those who noisily turn the pages of painted books, those who have in their power the black ink and the red ink, the paintings, they take us, they guide us, they show us the way."

It was important that she and her children knew the same things to be able to speak about the same things, to walk down the same paths. Perhaps if she and Jaramillo had not gone through the same events it would be difficult for them to understand what the conquest had been. Malinalli wanted the same complicity between her and her children and because of this she was willing to learn to read and write Spanish.

In the mornings, with Martín, she forced herself to scribble letters and numbers. The one that caught her attention was the number eight. She felt that it was the symbol of mixed ancestry. There were two circles united by the center, through the same invisible point, forever within each other.

In the afternoons, she liked to play with her children, grab them by their feet and spin them through the air, like her grandmother had done with her. When she got tired, she let them play by themselves and sat down to embroider *huipiles* as her children kept running around and Jaramillo, her husband, dedicated himself to carving wood.

Malinalli considered embroidering and wood carving more than just artisan activities; each was an exercise that nourished patience. Patience was the science of silence, where rhythm and harmony flowed naturally from stitch to stitch, from hammer to chisel. It was through such ritualistic and quotidian exercise that both were able to achieve luminous states of consciousness, where inner peace and spiritual richness were their objective and reward.

That afternoon, while they drank tea made from orange leaves, Jaramillo stopped working on a carving of the Virgin of Guadalupe for the children's bedroom.

"Marina," he asked. "Do you want to go to Mass tomorrow?"

"No. Do you want to go?"

"No."

Every year, a Mass was celebrated for the fall of Tenochtitlán. Malinalli did not like to go. She didn't like to bring back to mind the dead, the weeping, the crying. But what really bothered her was that the prayers were said before a crucified Christ, before the image of the new god, the god whose flesh was nailed to wood, the god with the bloodied body. It was horrifying for her to see it, for her mind had always rejected human sacrifices. It bothered her that the wound on the side reminded her of the wound made by obsidian knives in the chests of the men sacrificed in the temple of Huitzilopochtli. The crown of thorns bothered her also, and the dry coagulated blood. It made her want to save that man from the torment, to free him. She couldn't stand to look at him. His sacrifice was eternal and it spoke to the fact that, in spite of the conquest, there had been no change in these lands. The fall of the empire had meant nothing. The ritual of sacrifice had survived and it would be the heritage of those that remained. That Christ on the cross was pain without end. He was death eternal. Malinalli did not believe that the sacrifice had created light, let alone that light could have been found within such a sacrifice.

So she would rather not attend the ceremony and not see the sacrificed Christ. She would rather see life than death. She would rather see her children, products of the conquest, and not bring back the dead. She would rather kiss Jaramillo, love him and bless him, than to have to bless an image of eternal sacrifice. Thanks to Jaramillo she had found peace, heaven on earth; thanks to Cortés, war, exile, and hate. His presence gave rise to an uncontrollable disappointment. To see him unnerved her, bothered her, angered her. Inevitably, they would end up arguing.

⊷◄⊱⊰►⊶

That afternoon, he had shown up at their house and shattered a delightful day. They offered him a cup of chocolate with vanilla and invited him to sit with them by one of the fountains. Cortés, as always, had problems he wished to discuss. He was about to face a trial, in which he was charged with infidelity to the crown, tyrannous intentions, disobedience of royal orders, arbitrary crimes, and cruelty during the war; the failure to give the King of Spain what was due to him, the wrongful appropriation of large parcels of urban and rural lands, and the murder—among others— of Catalina Xuárez, his wife.

Confronted with the gravity of the accusations, Cortés had given the names of Malinalli and Jaramillo so that they could make declarations as his witnesses. By his tone in addressing them, Malinalli felt as if Cortés were not simply asking them, but had come to collect old debts. Cortés, aside from giving them the land where they now lived, had given them parcels in the towns of Oluela and Jaltipan, towns near Coatzacoalcos, where Malinalli was born. They had much to be grateful to him for; primarily, that he had married them. But Malinalli did not like the way in which he was demanding loyalty.

"And what do you want from me? To lie?"

"No, I expect you to be loyal."

Suddenly the afternoon acquired a gray cast and the sun was devoured by the humidity in the sky. Malinalli's eyes were wet, beautiful, and sorrowful; as if tired of looking, they wanted to silence the images in the brain and erase from memory all shapes and all reflections of a conquest and a deceitful illusory world. Pronouncing the word Cortés in a grave tone, she said:

"Cortés, I will forever be grateful for my son and the husband that you gave me, the piece of land that you kindly gave to Jaramillo and me so that we might spread our roots, but do not ask me to speak on your behalf, not in that tone. I am no longer your tongue, Lord Malinche."

It had been a long time since anyone had called him Malinche. They had stopped calling him that when Malinalli married Jaramillo, when she stopped being his woman, when they separated. Fire came out of his eyes and in a contained rage he responded:

"Who do you think you are, speaking to me like that?"

Jaramillo, who knew his wife better than anyone, saw the fit of anger in her eyes and he realized that she was going to vomit all of her hatred on Cortés. Excusing himself, he got up, took the children by the hand, and led them to their rooms.

Malinalli waited before answering Cortés. First she put together all the words that she had gathered in her moments of pain and desperation. She was tired, extremely tired of Cortés and all his strategies. She was tired of being his reflection. It was true, she could be his best witness, but what could she declare that wouldn't harm him? She, the most humble, the blindest of all, what could she have seen? She took a deep breath and spoke slowly.

"The worst of all the sicknesses born of your ambition hasn't been smallpox, or syphilis. The worst of all sicknesses are your cursed mirrors. Their light wounds like your sharp blade wounds, like your cruel words wound, like the balls of fire that spit from your cannons over my people wound. You brought your clear, silver, luminous mirrors. To see myself in them pains me, for the face that the mirror returns to me is not my own. It is an anguished and guilty face, a face covered by your kisses and marked by your bitter caresses. Your mirrors reflect back to me the fright of open grimaces in the face of men who have lost their language, their gods. Your mirrors reflect the stone without the volcano, the future without the tree. Your mirrors are like dry wells, empty, without spirit and eternity. In the images of your mirrors there are wails and crimes devoured by time. Your mirrors distort and drive mad whoever looks at themselves in them; they infect them with fear, they deform their hearts, destroy them, bleed them, and curse them. They deceive with their elusive, breakable, false spirit. Looking at yourself for long in your mirrors has made you ill, has shown you a mistaken glory and power. But worst of all is the fact that the face that you look at in the mirror—thinking that it is your face—does not exist; your mirrors have made it vanish and in its place you see a hallucinatory hell. Hell! That word I learned from you, that word that I do not understand, that place created by your people to eternally damn everything that lives. That terrifying universe that you have fabricated is the one that cuts out your image and freezes itself in the mirror. Your mirrors are as terrible as you are! What I most hate, Hernán, is to have looked at myself in your mirrors, in your black mirrors."

❖❖❖

The search for the gods is the search for oneself. And where do we find ourselves hidden? In the water, in the air, in the fire, in the earth. We are in the water, hidden in the river. Water makes up part of our body, but we do not see it; it courses through our veins, but we do not feel it. We only see the water on the outside. We only recognize ourselves in our reflections. When we look at ourselves in the water, we know too that we are light or we would not be reflected. We are fire, we are sun. We are in the air, in the word. When we say the names of our gods, we say our own. They created us with their word and we re-create them with ours. Gods and men are the same. Child of the sun, child of the water, child of the air, child of the corn; born in the womb of Mother Earth. When one finds the sun, the moving fire, the water, the hidden river, the air, the sacred song, the earth, and the flesh of corn within oneself, one is transformed into a god.

For Malinalli it was urgently necessary to find herself once again, by finding once again her gods. After the terrible argument with Cortés the previous day, she felt as if she wasn't inside her own body, that her soul had escaped, that it had fled, that it had evaporated with the rays of the sun. To see herself reflected in Hernán Cortés had left her confused. She had to confront her dark side before recapturing the light. To achieve this, she had to take the same journey that Quetzalcóatl had taken through the inner earth, through the underworld, before becoming the Morning Star. The cycle of Venus was the cycle of purification and rebirth. At a certain moment, Venus-Quetzalcóatl disappears, is not seen in the sky because he enters the womb of Mother Earth, he descends to recover the bones of his ancestors. Bones are the seed, the origin of the human body planted in the cosmos. Before recovering his body, Quetzalcóatl has to face his desires, see himself in the black mirror to achieve purification. If he is able to do it, the sun under the earth, under the hills, will lend its strength so that the earth opens and lets sprout the seed that is nourished with water from the hidden river. Quetzalcóatl, who descended as a fleshless spirit, in contact with the forces that bring forth life, will reunite his bones with his flesh.

Malinalli spent all night preparing for the journey. At dawn, she said goodbye to Jaramillo, her dear husband, and entrusted him with taking care of the children while she went in search of herself on the hill of Tepeyac. She felt aching, wounded. She felt that by attacking Cortés she had attacked herself. As she climbed the hill, she said: Water does not attack water. Corn does not attack corn. Air does not attack air. The earth does not attack the earth. It is the man who doesn't see himself in them that attacks them, destroys them. The man who attacks himself does away with the water, with the corn, with the earth, and stops saying the names of his gods. The man who doesn't see that his brother is also wind, also water, also corn, also air, cannot see god.

Malinalli wanted to see Tonantzin, the feminine deity, the Mother. She wanted to say her name to be part of her, to be able to look into her children's eyes without the fear of seeing anger reflected in them. She knew that to achieve integration with the forces of nature, of the cosmos, the first thing she had to do is keep silent and turn her heart toward heaven, full of devotion. Tepeyac, according to the tradition of her ancestors, was where Tonantzin could be found, but Malinalli was not sure where.

"Where are you?" she asked in silence. "Where are you, soul of things, essence of the visible, eternity of the stars? Where can I search in order to find you, if you are forbidden, if they have made you disappear, if they have ripped you from our faith, if they have tried to erase you from our memory?"

As she formulated these questions, she received the answers. It was truly as if, on the moment of thinking about her, she had entered into communication with Tonantzin. She heard in her mind that the essence of Tonantzin had returned to the depths of the mirror, the depths of the water, to be renewed as well. She too required it. In the deepest earth she had undone her appearance, her word, her touch, her strength. Now she was wind, water, fire, earth contained in a seed, and would soon reappear in new garments, a new form. She would arise from the dreams, the desires, the voices of those who summoned her, who remembered her. She would appear when her people awoke from the dream of death they had sunken into, the deceitful dream that made them believe that the reflection of their body had been erased from the sky. When they recovered their faith in the forces of nature, of creation, along with her they could paint her spirit. She would come dressed in the rays of the sun, sustained by the moon, in midair. Trembling in the wind, in a new shape, since the transformation of man, the transformation of the world, is the transformation of the universe. The Mexicas had changed, and so had the gods.

Our rituals would change in form, our language would become another, our prayers others, our communication different—Tonantzin told Malinalli—but the ancient gods, the immovable ones, the gods of all things, those that have no beginning and no end, will only change in form.

After listening to these words, Malinalli felt as if the air around her became perfumed, making evident the presence of the sacred. It was in the stillness of her mind that she had established contact with Tonantzin, and in the same manner she now addressed her reverently.

"To you, silence of the morning, perfume of thought, heart of desire, luminous intention of creation; to you, who give rise to the caresses of flowers, and who are the light of hope, the secret of the lips, the design of the invisible; to you I entrust that which I love, I entrust my children, who were born from the love that knows no flesh, who were born from the love that has no beginning, who were born from the noble, from the sacred; to you, who are one with them, I entrust them, so that you will dwell in their minds, guide their steps, inhabit their words, so that they never grow sick from their feelings, so that they never lose the will to live. Of you, dear mother, I ask that you be their reflection, so that on seeing you, they feel pride, they who do not belong to my world or to the Spaniards', they who are a mixture of all bloods—Iberian, African, Roman, Gothic, Native, and Middle Eastern—they, who along with all those now being born are the new vessel whereby the true thought of Christ-Quetzalcóatl is installed again in the hearts of men and casts its light on the world. Let them never be afraid! Never feel alone! Present yourself to them in your jade necklace, in your quetzal feathers, in your blanket of stars, so that they may recognize you and feel your presence. Protect them from illness; let the wind and the clouds sweep away all danger, all evil that pursues them. Don't allow them to gaze into a black mirror that tells them they are inferior, not worthy, that they should accept mistreatment and violence as their only due. Make sure that they never come to know treason, or hatred, or power, or ambition. Appear to them in their dreams so that the dream of war never establishes itself in their heads, that dream of collective madness, that sorrowful hell. Heal their fears, erase their fears, make them vanish, flee, drift away; erase all their fears along with mine, dear mother. That is what I ask of you, Great Lady. Strengthen the spirit of the new race that with new eyes looks on itself in the mirror of the moon, so that they may know that their presence on the earth is a fulfilled promise of the universe, a promise of plenty, of life, of redemption, and of love."

⊰⊱•❦•⊰⊱

This was Mexico and Malinalli knew it. When she finished her prayer, she took off the necklace of ceramic beads with the image of the lady Tonantzin—which was always hanging on her chest. It was the same one that her grandmother had given her when she was a girl. She also took out her rosary, the one she had made with the grains of corn with which, years before, her fate had been read to her. She buried both and with them buried her mother, her grandmother, herself and all the daughters of the corn. She asked the mother Tonantzin to nourish those grains with the waters from her hidden river, to help them bear fruit, to allow them to be food for the new beings that populated the Valley of Anáhuac.

Not knowing why, she remembered the Virgin of Guadalupe, that dark Virgin whose image Jaramillo and she had hung over their headboard. She was a revered virgin in the region of Extremadura, Spain. Jaramillo told her that the original image of the virgin was carved in black wood and showed the Virgin Mary with the Child God in her arms. Jaramillo carved a reproduction for her and as he did he told her that during the Arab conquest of Spain, the Spanish friars, fearing a desecration of the Virgin Mary, had buried her near the shores of the Guadalupe River—a name that was the Castilian rendering of the Arab *wad al luben*—and that meant *hidden river*. So when, years later, a pastor found her buried they named her after the river, the Virgin of Guadalupe.

That day Malinalli, seated on the hill of Tepeyac, after having buried her past, found herself, knew she was god, knew that she was eternal and that she was going to die, and that what gave life also died. She was at the apex of the hill. The wind blew in such a fashion that it almost knocked down the trees. The leaves fell away from them, filling her ear with music. The sound of the wind became clear. Malinalli felt the force of the wind on her face, her hair, over all her body and the heart of the sky opened itself for her.

Death did not frighten her. Everything around her spoke of change, of transformation, of rebirth. Tenochtitlán had died and in its place a new city rose that was ceasing to be a mirror, converting itself into earth and stone. Cortés had left off being a conquistador, and was becoming the Marquis of the Valley of Oaxaca. And she was soon going to experience her last transformation. She accepted it gladly. She knew that she would always belong to the universe, would change shape, but continue to exist. She would be in the water where her children played, in the stars Jaramillo watched at night, in the corn tortillas that they ate daily, in the wind that held up the hummingbirds that danced around their spikenard. She would exist in the streets of the new city, in what had been the market of Tlatelolco, in the woods of Chapultepec, in the sound of drums, in the seashells, in the snow of the volcanoes, in the sun, in the moon.

Malinalli, seated and in silence, became one with the fire, with the water, with the earth. She dissolved in the wind, knew she was in everything and in nothing. Nothing could contain her, or make her suffer. There was no grief, no rancor, only the infinite. She remained in that state until the birds announced that they would be taking the afternoon away with them among their feathers.

When Malinalli returned to be by her husband and children, she looked different. She radiated peace. She embraced them tightly and kissed them, then played with her children before putting them to bed. She made love to her husband all night. Then, she went out to the patio and by the light of the moon and a torch, a sun and a moon, she tried to express in one image the experience of that magical day. She opened her codex and painted the luminous lady Tonantzin, the protector, covering with her blanket the house where her family was sleeping. Afterward, she washed her brushes in one of the fountains in the patio.

The silence was complete.

She breathed in the aroma of the spikenard, put her feet in the water, walked through the middle of the canal, and reached the center of the patio. There, she entered into the center of the Cross of Quetzalcóatl, the center of all crossroads, where the Cihuateteo, the women who had died during childbirth, who made up the entourage of the women who follow Tlazolteotl, Coatlicue, and Tonantzin, the different manifestations of the same feminine deity, appeared; and there, in the center of the Universe, Malinalli became liquid.

She was water of the moon.

Malinalli, like Quetzalcóatl before her, on facing her dark side, became aware of the light. Her will was to be one with the cosmos, and she forced the limits of her body to disappear. Her feet, in contact with the water, bathed by the moonlight, were the first to experience the transformation. They no longer held her. Her spirit became one with the water. It scattered in the air. Her skin expanded to the limit, allowing her to change shape and become one with everything that surrounded her. She was spikenard, she was orange tree, she was stone, she was aroma of copal, she was corn, she was fish, she was bird, she was sun, she was moon. She abandoned this world.

At that moment, a bolt of lightning, a silver tongue, lit the sky, heralding a storm and filling with light the still body of Malinalli, who had died instantaneously some moments before. Her eyes were absorbed by the stars, which immediately knew everything that she had seen on the earth.

On that thirteenth day of the month, Malinalli was born to eternity. Juan Jaramillo celebrated it in his own way. He brought together his children in the patio, which they filled with flower and song. Then they each read a poem written for Malinalli in Náhuatl. When the ritual was over, they remained silent in order to become impregnated by Malinalli before going to sleep.

In contrast with this simple ceremony, on that same date, the colonial authorities organized a great feast to commemorate the fall of Tenochtitlán, on the thirteenth of August in 1521. The celebration took place in the church of San Hipólito, since the date that marked the Spanish victory over the natives was the same as the day of that saint.

Jaramillo was invited to attend the celebratory Mass of the fall of Tenochtitlán several times, and several times he declined. Years later, they granted him the honor of carrying the banner during the feast of St. Hipólito—which commemorated the Spanish triumph over Tenochtitlán—but he declined, which the authorities took as an affront.

ACKNOWLEDGMENTS

In the air, in the invisible, an infinity of ideas flow. During their journey they cross one another and create luminous encounters that later shape themselves into images, sounds, words: into knowledge.

This book is a result of my search for answers to the questions: Who was Malinche? What did she think? What did she know? What were her thoughts?

I found the answers not only in books but in conversations with my friends and in my contact with the invisible, where time vanishes and it is possible to have lucky encounters with the past.

For this journey I tried on the company and unconditional support of Javier Valdés, who helped me with the work of investigation, of Salvador Garcini, who joined this effort and shared with us his dreams, of Antonio Velasco Piña, who enriched our knowledge of Mexico's history.

Victor Medina and Soledad Ruiz made many invaluable suggestions.

My nephew Jordi Castells added his talent, his intuition, and his sensibility with the creation of the codex that accompanies this edition.

My brother Julio Esquivel and Juan Pablo Villaseñor gave me their time and their guidance through cyberspace in the gathering of facts.

Cristina Barros and Marcos Buerosto joined in with their knowledge of Mexican cuisine.

To all I extend my heartfelt gratitude.

BIBLIOGRAPHY

Argüelles, José. *El factor Maya*. Hoja Casa Editorial. Mexico, 1993.

Cortés, Hernán. *Cartas de relación*. Editorial Porrúa, nineteenth edition. Mexico, 2002.

Carrillo de Albornoz, José Miguel. *Moctezuma, el semidiós destronado*. Editorial Planeta Mexicana, S.A. de C.V., first reprint (Mexico): January, 2005.

Díaz del Castillo, Bernal. *Historia verdadera de la conquista de la Nueva España*. Editorial Porrúa, twentieth edition. Mexico, 2002.

Díaz Infante, Fernando. *La educación de los aztecas*. Panorama Editorial, fifth reprint. Mexico, 2001.

Durán, Fray Diego. *Historia de las Indias de Nueva España e islas de la tierra firme*. Editorial Porrúa, second edition. Mexico, 1984.

———. *Ritos y fiestas de los antiguos mexicanos*. Editorial Cosmos, first edition. Mexico, 1980.

Escalante Plancarte, Salvador. *Fray Martín de Valencia*. Editorial Cossio. Mexico, 1945.

Fernández del Castillo, Francisco. *Catalina Xuárez Marcayda*. Editorial Cosmos, first edition. Mexico, 1980.

Florescano, Enrique. *El mito de Quetzalcóatl*. Fondo de Cultura Económica, third reprint. Mexico, 2000.

Fuentes Mares, José. *Cortés, el hombre*. Editorial Grijalbo. Mexico, 1981.

Glantz, Margo (Coordinadora). *La Malinche, sus padres y sus hijos*. Taurus. Mexico, 2001.

Gómez de Orozco, Federico. *Doña Marina, la dama de la conquista*. Ediciones Xochitl. Mexico, 1942.

Guerrero, José Luis. *Flor y canto del nacimiento de México*. Librería Parroquial de Clavería, first edition. Mexico, 1990.

Gutiérrez Contreras, Francisco. *Hernán Cortés*. Salvat Editores. Barcelona, 1986.

Herren, Ricardo. *Doña Marina, la Malinche*. Editorial Planeta, third reprint. Mexico, 1994.

Lanyon, Anna. *La conquista de la Malinche*. Editorial Diana. Mexico, 2001.

León Portilla, Miguel. *Toltecáyotl, aspectos de la cultura Náhuatl*. Fondo de Cultura Económica, fifth reprint. Mexico, 1995.

Martín del Campo, Marisol. *Amor y conquista: la novela de Malinalli, mal llamada la Malinche*. Editorial Planeta/ Joaquín Mortiz. Mexico, 1999.

————. *Doña Marina*. Editorial Planeta de Agostini. Mexico, 2002.

Martinez, José Luis. *Hernán Cortés* (versión abreviada). Fondo de Cultura Económica, first reprint. Mexico, 1995.

Menéndez, Miguel Angel. *Malintzin, en un fuste, seis rostros y una sola máscara*. Editora de Periódicos S.C.L. "La Prensa," first edition. Mexico, 1964.

Miralles, Juan. *La Malinche*. Tusquets Editores México S.A. de C.V. , first edition. Mexico, 2004.

Moctezuma, Hipólito. *Astrología Azteca*. Ediciones Obelisco. Barcelona, 2000.

Nuñes Becerra, Fernanda. *La Malinche: de la historia al mito*. Instituto Nacional de Antropología e Historia. Col. Divulgación, second reprint. Mexico, 2002.

Pradier, Kay. *La princesse aztèque Malinalli*. Éditions Favre. Lausanne, 2001.

Prescott, W. H. *Historia de la conquista de México*. Editorial Porrúa. Mexico, 1976.

Rascón Banda, Víctor Hugo. *La Malinche*. Plaza & Janés. Mexico, 2000.

Ruiz de Velasco y T., Luis. *Malinche, el Teule*. Editorial Planeta. Mexico, 1995.

Sahagún, Fray Bernadino de. *Historia General de las cosas de la Nueva España*. Editorial Porrúa, tenth edition. Mexico, 1999.

Séjourné, Laurette. *Pensamiento y religión en el México Antiguo*. Fondo de Cultura Económica, ninth reprint. Mexico, 1990.

————. *El universo de Quetzalcóatl*. Fondo de Cultura Económica, fifth reprint. Mexico, 1998.

Thomas, Hugh. *Conquest: Montezuma, Cortés, and the Fall of Old Mexico*. Touchstone. New York, 1995.

Valle-Arizpe, Artemio de. *Andanzas de Hernán Cortés*. Editorial Diana, first edition. Mexico, 1978.

ABOUT THE AUTHOR

Laura Esquivel was born in Mexico City in 1950. Her first novel, *Like Water for Chocolate* (1989), stayed on the *New York Times* bestseller list for over one year, has been translated into more than thirty-three languages, and has sold about three million copies around the world. The film, based on the novel, with a script written by Esquivel herself, not only won several prizes but was an impressive box-office success. Laura Esquivel lives in Mexico.

MALINCHE

⬤≪K ≫⬤

Laura Esquivel

A Readers Club Guide

In *Malinche*, Laura Esquivel reimagines the relationship between the Spaniard Hernán Cortés and the Indian woman Malinalli, his interpreter and mistress during his conquest of the Aztecs. Malinalli meets Cortés and, like many, including the Aztec king Montezuma, suspects that he is the returning forefather god of their tribe, Quetzalcóatl. She assumes that her task is to welcome Cortés/Quetzalcóatl and help him destroy the Aztec empire and free her people, but she gradually comes to realize that Cortés's thirst for conquest is all too human.

Throughout Mexican history, Malinalli has been reviled for her betrayal of the Indian people. But recent historical research has shown that her role was much more complex. She was the mediator between two cultures, Hispanic and Native American, and three languages, Spanish, Mayan, and Náhuatl. She was also a slave, trying to rebel against the barbarous culture of her masters, the Aztecs. But her loyalty was to her own people, whom she was trying to set free.

Laura Esquivel challenges the traditional mythology through a character-driven portrait of the Adam and Eve of mestizo culture, Cortés and Malinalli, with the backdrop of the fall of the Aztec Empire. Told with the lyricism of the Náhuatl song tradition and pictorial language, Esquivel gives us a creation myth of the new-world hybrid culture and a legendary affair.

GROUP DISCUSSION QUESTIONS

1. Laura Esquivel dedicated *Malinche* to the wind. What does this symbolize, and what other dedications would be appropriate for this book?

2. Other than Malinalli's affair with Cortés and her eventual marriage to Jaramillo, the relationships she has in the book are maternal. Discuss the themes represented by Malinalli as granddaughter, daughter, and mother.

3. How did you feel about the drawings, which represent Malinalli's telling of the story, at the beginning of each chapter? Did you realize they were codices? Were you able to "read" them? Did they enhance your understanding of the story?

4. Malinalli's father tells her, "Your word will have eyes and will see, will have ears and will hear, will have the tact to lie with the truth and to tell truths that will seem like lies" (page 9). To what extent was her father's prayer realized?

5. What forms of power might a translator have? Which ones did Malinalli have as a woman and a slave? Which ones do you think she used or was tempted to use? Was she aware of her own power?

6. Malinalli finds meaning in the Christian rituals, linking them to her culture's stories and deities. Were you surprised at how easily she was able to embrace both traditions?

7. Which rituals and symbols are common to both the indigenous Indian religion and to Christianity? How does your own faith affect your response to Malinalli?

8. Toward the end of the tale, Malinalli questions the role of human sacrifice and the loss of life in war. Would a woman of that time and status have such progressive ideas? Discuss other times in the novel where she demonstrates such forward thinking. When does she not?

9. History and fiction intertwine in any work of historical fiction. As you read *Malinche*, did you find yourself wondering which details were historical and which were the fruit of the author's imagination?

10. How do you think the derogatory usage of the word "Malinche" affected the author's desire to reimagine Malinalli's story?

11. Malinalli says, "The search for the gods is the search for oneself" (page 178). How does faith, the pursuit of meaning, and the desire to understand deity frame this novel?

12. Ultimately, how do you view Malinalli? As a traitor, a martyr, or as a heroine?

TIPS TO ENHANCE YOUR BOOK CLUB

1. Review the images from the front of the book. As a group, create a codex (storytelling through images) of a recent event in your group or town, utilizing sketches, photographs, or symbols but no words or letters. Or each group member could create a codex, which the rest of the group could then attempt to "read."

2. Identify a restaurant or cookbook that specializes in traditional foods of Mexico, such as Rick Bayless's *Mexican Chicken*. (simonsays.com/content/book.cfm?sid=33&pid=405956). Share a meal together that highlights the Indian and Spanish ingredients Malinalli features in her new mestizo dishes.

3. Purchase postcards or look online for the flag of modern-day Mexico and find out what the central image signifies. (Hint: It determined the site of Tenochtitlán.)

4. Seek an opportunity to further understand Malinalli's world by visiting a museum or art exhibit together.

5. Laura Esquivel is a screenwriter, and her first novel became the award-winning film *Like Water for Chocolate*. Discuss how you would film her novel *Malinche*. If you have read *Like Water for Chocolate*, which themes do you see repeated in *Malinche?*

A CONVERSATION WITH
LAURA ESQUIVEL

1. *What prompted you to write this novel?*

   The editors at a publishing house in Spain got in touch with me and suggested I write a biographical novel about Malinche's life. I loved the idea and that's how the project got started. Of course, it turned out to be more difficult than I was expecting. I spent two years doing research and my husband, Javier Valdés, helped me with this arduous task.

2. *How much time did you devote to the book? What historical sources did you use in your research?*

   There is actually very little information on Malinche. What we know about her comes from the historical chronicles of the period, which don't total more than a few pages. So my job was to try to imagine what Malinche was like, how she thought, how she interpreted what she witnessed, because I find it interesting that people see the world not as it is, but rather as they are. Taking this into account, it is essential to analyze someone's belief system before judging their behavior. In making a novel out of her life, of course I had to use real events as the basis, and that's where I had to immerse myself in the history, religious thought, and the astronomical, cosmic, and biological knowledge of the period in which Malinche lived.

3. *There are numerous theories about Malinalli's death; among them, that she was murdered. Why did you choose this end for Malinalli? Why bring Malinalli to Tepeyac Hill?*

Because Tepeyac is where Tonantzin, the quintessential mother figure, is worshipped. And because in that same spot, on the twelfth day of the twelfth month, twelve years after Cortés's arrival, the Virgin of Guadalupe, the symbol of cultural and religious syncretism, would appear. I put Malinche there just hours before her death, entrusting her children to Tonantzin, on a twelfth day, the same day that Malinalli was born, as a way of closing, with her, a female cycle of regeneration and life.

4. *What does* malinche *mean in the Náhuatl language? Explain the significance of this word. How strong is the resonance of the word* malinche *today in Mexico? When is it used and by whom?*

Malinche is the name the indigenous people gave to Cortés, because it was similar to Malinalli, which was Malinche's real name. I don't know exactly at what point Malinalli became Malinche and Cortés was no longer called Malinche. Malinalli is a plant, a twisted climbing vine that was used for building houses, but it was also an astrological sign. Today, *malinche* is used pejoratively to describe someone who denies their heritage, someone who values other cultures above their own.

5. *Malinche is considered by some to be a traitor. What is your opinion of her?*

Historical facts cannot be judged from a modern perspective. When Cortés arrived in the New World, Mexico as we know it did not exist. There was an empire that had imposed itself by force and from which everyone wanted to escape. Malinche was a slave who before being given to Cortés had already been given away twice before. She had no obligation to be loyal to an empire that had subjugated everyone, with no respect for their rights. But that was not the most important thing; what is most relevant is the way in which she carried out her job as the "tongue," as the mediator between two worlds, between two visions.

6. *What did Malinalli give to you, as a writer? What did you learn from interpreting history through the eyes of this native woman?*

It was a pleasant experience, because the indigenous peoples have a wonderful vision of the cosmos, of the Earth, and of nature's forces. If only we could recover that sacred connection with the world that surrounds us. For our ancestors, every daily task had a meaning that went far beyond simple personal satisfaction. They knew that everything has an effect on everything else. There is nothing that we say, think, or do that goes unnoticed. And now, thanks to the latest discoveries in quantum physics, we know what this means. In these absurdly materialistic times, awakening our cosmic awareness would be a real alternative.

7. *Malinalli went from being a slave to becoming the most powerful woman in the conquest. Where does this ambition, if you can call it that, come from in her?*

Malinche was driven by a desire for freedom, something very different from the ambition that motivated Cortés. Someone given as a slave three times, who had to "conquer" her masters in order to be treated well, must have nurtured inside herself the desire to be someone special. To be treated better. To be appreciated. When Cortés offers her freedom in exchange for her work as a translator, that automatically gives her power. The power to translate. The power of the word. The power to control information.

8. *Malinalli gave rise to the Mexican people by giving birth to a half-indigenous and half-Spanish son. What does it mean that Malinalli, thanks to the double meaning of the word, wraps him up twice, both with her body and with the cloth woven of malinalli?*

The Aztec hieroglyph that represents the twelfth day— the day that marks Malinche's destiny—has a skull in profile. Instead of hair, the skull has *malinalli*, the fiber also known as coalman's grass. It is the symbol of that which dies and is transformed. It also alludes to a new people, snatched from the jaws of death by their mother, who wrapped them in *malinalli* in order to make them whole again, with new life. Malinche wrapping up her son with her own body has all of these meanings.

9. *Let's talk a little bit about the separate spheres within the novel; there is the sphere ruled by the Náhuatl*

and the one the Spaniards dominate, so there is an indigenous realm and a European one, neither of which has room for those of mixed race.

Throughout the conquest and for many years following it, the indigenous world was devalued, the European overvalued and the mestizo, or mixed race, had a conflicted, divided identity. Reconsidering the conquest allows one to see the indigenous world in a different way and, of course, the mestizo world as well. This new position shifts the idealized European world into a more realistic light and allows people of mixed race to see themselves in a more comfortable way, and even proudly.

10. *Tell us about the cult of the Virgin of Guadalupe and the pyramid of Tonantzin. What significance do they have today in your country?*

The cult of the Virgin of Guadalupe is the most important in my country. Each year, her shrine is visited by millions of pilgrims, and the holiday devoted to celebrating her includes pagan rituals dedicated to Tonantzin. One could say that before we were Mexicans, we were Guadalupans. The Virgin of Guadalupe was the most important cohesive factor, second only to the conquest. The image of the virgin came to us from Europe but it contains a series of absolutely clear syncretic indigenous elements, which blend two cosmologies into one. This attempt at cultural and spiritual reconciliation is one of the most important elements of the unifying spirit of the Mexican people: our mixed heritage. All of us mestizos are survivors of the conquest and we all must accommodate two, or more, cultures in order to exist.

11. *If Malinalli had left texts or documents such as codices, what would they have said?*

That is exactly the question I asked myself, and the answer lies in the codex that accompanies this book. In it, I tried to capture the images that Malinche would have painted to tell her story. Jordi Castells created the codex, and in order to do so he had to carry out an intense period of research on pre-Hispanic codices. The result is excellent.